Big Love in a Small Town

Kate Goldman

Big Love in a Small Town

Published by Kate Goldman

Copyright © 2015 by Kate Goldman

ISBN 978-1-50847-333-6

First printing, 2015

All rights reserved. No part of this book may be reproduced in any form or by any electronic or mechanical means including information storage and retrieval systems – except in the case of brief quotations in articles or reviews – without the permission in writing from its publisher, Kate Goldman.

www.KateGoldmanBooks.com

PRINTED IN THE UNITED STATES OF AMERICA

Dedication

I want to dedicate this book to my beloved husband, who makes every day in my life worthwhile. Thank you for believing in me when nobody else does, giving me encouragement when I need it the most, and loving me simply for being myself.

Table of Contents

CHAPTER 1 1

CHAPTER 2 19

CHAPTER 3 41

CHAPTER 4 54

CHAPTER 5 64

CHAPTER 6 79

CHAPTER 7 96

CHAPTER 8 112

ONE LAST THING…..120

ABOUT KATE GOLDMAN 121

Chapter 1

As another tear plopped onto the keys of her laptop, Tessa Jacobson sighed in frustration. Was she ever going to stop crying? It sure didn't seem like it. Three weeks had passed since Davis had broken up with her and moved to Nashville with his band, and as each day came and went, Tessa still felt her heart continuing to break.

Tessa was crushed. According to Davis, it was for the best that they broke things off, and it wouldn't be good for either of them to attempt a long-distance relationship, but she completely disagreed. How could he so easily toss seven years together down the drain like that?

What compounded the pain was the fact that not only had he left her, but he was sharing a two-bedroom apartment with the rest of the band – including Shauna Reagan, their lead singer and a girl that Tessa never really liked.

Sure, Davis promised he still cared for her, that there was no one else involved in his decision to end things, and that the breakup was what was truly best for the both of them, but that didn't stop Tessa from fearing that Shauna had probably already sunk her claws into him. After all, Davis was a musician, and a good-looking one at that. Why wouldn't Shauna try to steal him away?

Big Love in a Small Town

I guess it isn't stealing – he isn't mine anymore, she thought as she dabbed her eyes with a tissue. After a deep breath to steady herself and a sip of hot tea, she attempted to finish the announcement currently filling her computer screen.

Tessa knew she was going to have to start pulling it together. She was at work, for goodness' sake, crying in her cubicle. Mr. Hart, the editor of *The Clearhill News* and her boss, had been understanding and tolerant so far, but the good people of Clearhill, Georgia, needed their newspaper three times a week, no matter what was going on in Tessa's personal life.

However, no matter how hard she tried to focus, the words just wouldn't come. How could she write up engagement announcements for several happy couples with her heart feeling like lead in her chest? She scanned through her other assignments, looking for something to work on that would better fit her current mood. She would just have to go back to the announcements later.

When she'd managed to get a couple of paragraphs into a write-up about an upcoming road closure, Tessa heard her phone vibrate from its place inside her top desk drawer. Her hopes rose for a fleeting second, hoping it would be Davis, even though he hadn't contacted her since the day he left. When would she ever quit hoping it was Davis?

It, of course, wasn't him, but Tessa was pleased to see that it was Natalie, her best friend since childhood, wanting to have lunch together in a little while. Natalie was a paralegal at a lawyer's office just two blocks from the newspaper.

This was one of the things Tessa loved about living in a small town – everything was in walkable distance, but the atmosphere was homey and cozy, unlike bigger cities. She'd studied journalism at Georgia State in downtown Atlanta, so she knew what it was like to live in both worlds, and moving back home to Clearhill had definitely been the perfect choice for her after she graduated. It would take something really special to get her to move back to a big city.

With her spirits livened a bit, she spent the rest of the morning pounding out the road closure article before leaving to meet Natalie at the Corner Café, their favorite place for lunch.

Scanning the crowded bistro, she spotted Natalie at a small table near the window. Natalie waved, and Tessa hurried over, draping her emerald-green pea coat over the back of the metal chair before sitting down.

"Hello, lady," Natalie said with a grin gracing her flawless face, pushing a cup of cinnamon hot chocolate, the Corner's signature drink, towards Tessa.

Tessa and Natalie, while both beautiful, were completely opposite in looks. Natalie was blonde, fair-skinned, tall and wafer thin, while Tessa was dark-haired with a peach complexion and a petite, hourglass figure.

"Quit trying so hard to cheer me up," Tessa muttered, but she couldn't help but smile after taking her first sip of the delicious warmth.

"Tessa, as your best friend since third grade, it's my job to cheer you up and remind you that this whole situation is really in your best interest," Natalie reminded her for what seemed like the twentieth time.

"I've heard you, Nat. Loud and clear – over and over. It still doesn't make it any easier. Davis and I were together for seven years, since our senior year of high school."

"You are wearing rose-colored glasses, honey. Are you counting your entire junior year of college when you two were broken up because you caught him cheating on you...red-handed? I think you're having selective memory issues, and I'm here to remind you of all of the bad stuff that you happen to be conveniently forgetting."

Natalie was, thankfully, the harsh dose of truth Tessa needed. Things with Davis hadn't been perfect, and it was good to be reminded of that quite often while in the midst of her current heartbreak.

Big Love in a Small Town

Tessa noticed the sun reflecting off the three-carat rock that graced Natalie's hand, courtesy of Natalie's perfectly wonderful fiancé. Of course, Tessa was beyond thrilled about her best friend's engagement, but she'd just lost a relationship with someone that had meant the world to her. Even if Davis wasn't always worth the love and affection she'd freely given him, it was impossible not to mourn the loss. It was easy for Natalie to point out how Tessa was much better off without Davis, but Natalie had someone to share life with, and Tessa was very much alone now.

After their food arrived, the conversation took a change for the better in Tessa's opinion. She was tired of talking about what was wrong with her love life. Camera crews were setting up just across the street on the town square's grassy lawn, providing the perfect distraction from their current topic of discussion.

"What do you think they're filming now?" Natalie asked, before taking a bite of her sandwich.

Tessa pushed her salad around, trying to remember what movies had been on the filming schedule that the town's Chamber of Commerce had sent over to the newspaper office. The chamber wanted the newspaper to keep the town's filming status front and center, so it was part of Tessa's job to know what was happening.

"I think it's a love story with Nate Wilder and Ansley Madison. The name of the movie, according to the list, is *In Her Arms*," Tessa finally remembered.

"Wow. They are really big stars. I wish Clearhill would have become the Hollywood of the South when we were teenagers and I had time to care more," Natalie replied, referencing the name Clearhill had taken on about a year ago, thanks to the numerous movies and television shows that were constantly filming in the area – especially downtown where she and Natalie worked and lived.

"I know, right? Between the newspaper and my shifts at The Grille, I don't have time for stargazing, but I sure wish I did."

"How's it going at The Grille?"

"Crazy busy. I make too much money to quit – even if I do hate serving."

"Yeah, I definitely miss the extra money, but I agree, being a waitress sucks," Natalie said. She had left The Grille three months earlier after getting a raise at the law firm. Tessa wasn't that lucky. The Grille was the nicest restaurant and bar in Clearhill, and the tips she earned in two evenings were sometimes more than her weekly pay at *The Clearhill News*.

Noticing that the lunch hour was quickly coming to an end, the girls finished up their lunch, and hurried back to work. Time always flew faster during lunch than it did during the rest of the day, but Tessa made sure to keep a close watch on the time since she did have to be at The Grille as soon as she closed the newspaper office at four.

A couple of minutes before it was time for her to leave, Tessa changed into her black shirt and pants so that she could power walk over to The Grille and get right into the swing of things once she arrived.

Despite the swift pace of her life at the moment, she was thankful that her two jobs kept her busy enough to keep her mind off of the fact that she was still getting over a terrible breakup. As long as she kept going, she figured at some point her heart would eventually start healing.

At the stroke of four, Tessa gathered her things, and sprinted out of the door, making sure to lock it behind her. She was the last one to leave on Fridays. Everyone else cut out at noon, but she used the extra time to proof her articles, and she enjoyed the peace and quiet.

The air had grown significantly colder as the afternoon waned into early evening, and when she burst into the restaurant's back kitchen door, she'd never been more thankful for the excessive warmth coming from the fired-up ovens and stove tops.

Tessa put her bag and coat on the shelf in the tiny storage closet and donned her little ruffled apron. She went to the small powder room and applied her favorite red lipstick, stuck in a pair of diamond studs that were a Christmas gift from her parents two years ago, and pulled her long, glossy hair into a sleek ponytail. She knew that looking good exponentially increased her take, especially during happy hour.

With one last turn to make sure she was presentable, Tessa headed out to the floor with the biggest smile she could muster plastered across her face. The crowd was already thick, with every high top and table in her section filled with locals who were thankful that the workday was over and were ready to get their weekend started.

A couple of hours into her shift, Tessa slipped into the kitchen to take a quick break. Of course, table nine still needed their bottle of Merlot, and twelve was waiting on their rib eyes, but with the rush of happy hour turning into the flurry of the Friday evening dinner crowd, if she didn't take a step back to breathe, at least one of her patrons was going to end up with their order in their lap and not on the table where it belonged.

"Come on, Tessa. We've got this. Only four more hours to go!" Natasha, another waitress, sarcastically joked as she picked up a couple of baskets of artisan bread.

Tessa smiled and shook her head, grabbing up the steaks that had come up while she had been hiding in the back of the kitchen, and headed back into the fray.

On and on the crazy pace went, every table packed, Tessa being tugged in twenty different directions nonstop, until, finally, around 10:30, the dinner rush was blessedly over. From that point until they closed at eleven, it would probably be pretty quiet, with only a few random guests coming in for desserts or drinks.

Tessa used the time to help the bartender restock, and to count and recount her totals. At ten minutes until closing, all she could think about was going home and drawing a nice warm bath. That is, until she saw, from her position behind the bar, that the hostess was leading someone to her section.

Damn, she thought. There went the possibility of her leaving on time tonight. Tessa ducked into the kitchen to grab a basket of bread for her guest. Better to get on top of things quickly, and hope that she could get out of here before midnight.

The man seated in her section had his back to the kitchen; but as Tessa walked towards the table where he was seated, she could tell that he wasn't from Clearhill. He was definitely either part of the filming crew or an actor – they had a more polished, yet edgy style that was unlike anything she'd seen before in her small town. It wasn't that the Clearhill townspeople weren't put together or anything, it's just that the film industry folks were different – different but cool.

Maybe staying late won't be so terrible, after all, Tessa mused. She was actually kind of excited to get to interact with someone from one of the movie sets.

"Hi, my name is Tessa and I'll be your server tonight. Can I start you off with something to drink?" Tessa had the hardest time getting through her normal spiel when she realized that not only was she serving someone from the set, she was waiting on Nate Wilder, one of the most well-known, up-and-coming actors in Hollywood.

Keep it together, keep it together, she inwardly chanted. The last thing she wanted was to come across as a crazy fan. She only mildly followed celebrity gossip – just the random perusal through a magazine while waiting in line to check out at the grocery store – but still, who wouldn't be slightly star-struck given the circumstances?

"Hi, Tessa, it's nice to meet you. Can you tell me what you have available on tap?" Nate responded with an easy smile. Tessa rattled off a list of The Grille's offerings as she took in his gorgeous, chiseled face, dark brown hair and piercing blue eyes. He was every bit as hot as every movie had made him out to be.

"I'll take the southern pecan ale – that sounds interesting," he replied after she had explained the different beers on tap.

Tessa laughed. "It's really good, I promise," she smiled, feeling more at ease the longer she was around him. She couldn't help but put emphasis on her description of the pecan ale when she listed the offerings – it was her favorite, and he must have picked up on that.

"I'm going to take your word for it," he joked back, giving her a wink.

Tessa headed to the bar to get his beer. She was immediately surrounded by three other servers.

"Is that Nate Wilder?" one of them asked.

Tessa nodded. "Y'all need to get it together. He is just a customer like any other, and we can't make him feel weird, or he won't ever come back," Tessa reminded them.

A moment later, Tessa set the tall pilsner glass in front of Nate, and hoped that he would like the craft beer as much as she did, especially since he ordered it off her subliminal recommendation.

"Thanks," he said and took a sip. "This is so good. I looked over the menu, but I think I'd rather you surprise me with whatever you suggest. I can trust your judgment now that I've tasted this," he said before taking another sip.

"Are you kidding me? What if you totally hate what I choose? The pecan beer is my favorite – everyone loves it – but food is a whole different ball game," Tessa replied, astounded.

"I'm not that picky, I promise," Nate laughed.

Tessa arched an eyebrow at him. She was still surprised that they were having such an easy conversation, and that the initial nervousness of serving a celebrity had dissipated.

"Alright then, I'll be back shortly with a crowd favorite." Tessa began to head for the kitchen.

"I'd rather have Tessa's favorite," Nate called out as she retreated.

Tessa stopped in her tracks. Was he flirting with her? She didn't know how she felt about this. He could have any girl he wanted – did he consider it a game to pick up random waitresses?

Tessa turned around to face him. "I'll bring you my favorite, then," she replied with a professional smile before continuing on to the kitchen where the cook staff waited with anticipation.

"What does he want for dinner?" the head chef, Art, burst out excitedly as soon as she entered the kitchen.

"He told me he wanted my favorite meal here," Tessa replied, still confused.

"Your favorite is the shrimp and grits, isn't it?" Art asked, already starting to gather ingredients, not caring in the least about the underlying meaning of the actor wanting Tessa's favorite dish. Tessa wasn't surprised that Art already knew her favorite, she ordered it pretty often.

"Yep, it is. Hope he isn't allergic to shellfish," Tessa said as she prepped a Caesar salad, her favorite pairing with shrimp and grits.

"What do you think it means that he wanted your favorite?" Natasha asked from her perch on a stool. She had already cashed out for the evening, but obviously wasn't leaving with such a famous person still in the building.

"I guess he wanted a suggestion," Tessa nonchalantly replied.

"Or he thinks you're hot," Natasha pointed out with a silly grin. Tessa playfully shoved Natasha, and rolled her eyes. There was no way Nate Wilder was interested in her. He was Nate Wilder, for crying out loud. He could have any girl he wanted and he probably knew it, which didn't make his attention seem all that appealing to Tessa.

"I'm just going to do my job and treat him the way I would treat any other customer," Tessa told Natasha as she squared her shoulders, and went back out to serve her famous guest.

Tessa had a feeling it was going to be a lot harder to act like she wasn't interested than she initially thought it would be as she took in the sight of Nate's face lighting up with a smile when he saw her coming. She felt her willpower instantly turn to mush.

"Hello, again," Nate commented as she placed the salad bowl on the table.

"Um, hi?" she ventured, unsure of how to respond to his flirty banter.

Tessa's uncertain question made Nate laugh. "You are a breath of fresh air, Tessa, and you don't even know it," he said on a more serious note.

"Thanks for the compliment, but I'm not sure what you mean by it."

"I've been flirting with you since the first moment we met and you either haven't noticed or you don't care," he pointed out.

Tessa thought for a moment before answering him. Should she be honest and risk pissing him off? She weighed the options before figuring she should just go with honesty. This whole experience so far had been surreal anyway.

"I did notice, and I do care. I care enough about myself to know that hopping into bed with you would be a monumental mistake," she replied frankly. Tessa knew this was definitely not the answer he was expecting, but she went ahead and laid her cards out on the table – she wasn't about to have her heart broken into even tinier pieces.

"Oh, I'm sorry, but you have it wrong. I apologize if I came off that way – I'm not like that at all. I've been acting this way because I'm genuinely interested in getting to know you. I don't know anyone around here, except for the cast and crew, and since we will be in the area for a few weeks, and tonight I was lucky enough to be seated in a beautiful and feisty woman's section, I thought it would be nice to hang out and maybe get to know one another," he explained, casting his eyes down.

Tessa felt guilty. She had gone and made assumptions about Nate that weren't founded. "I'm really sorry I jumped to conclusions like that – it's just you have to know where I'm coming from. You can hang out with anyone that you want to, have any girl in Hollywood, and you are hitting on a waitress in Clearhill? I assumed you were just looking for a one-night stand, so I wasn't about to let myself be drawn in – no matter how attractive you are," she told him.

"Well, now that we have gotten this awkward conversation out of the way, can I have your phone number?" he said after a few seconds, obviously rallied from her initial rejection.

"Are you kidding me? After all that I just said, and after basically assuming you were a sleazeball, you still want my number?" Tessa couldn't help but display her shock. Most guys would have run for the hills after this conversation.

"I like your frankness – most girls just tell me whatever they think I want to hear. You haven't done that, that's for sure," he quipped.

Tessa stared at him for a second before a giggle escaped her lips. Seriously? What was she doing? This gorgeous man was sharing playful banter with her and it was as if she was making it her personal goal to push him away.

With a new determination not to be such a Debbie Downer anymore, Tessa took out an empty ticket from the pocket of her apron and scribbled down her name and number.

"Here," she said, handing him the note, "I'm not sure if we can get our schedules to line up, but I'd love the chance to get to know you better, too."

When Nate took the paper from her, his fingers brushed over hers, and Tessa felt a ripple of involuntary attraction shoot through her body. At the unexpected turn of events, she decided now might be the best time to check on his order. She could feel a blush spreading across her cheeks.

"Are you free tonight?" Nate asked her just as she turned, thwarting her getaway.

"Ah, yes, I suppose I will be," she said, turning to face him again.

"Would you like to get a late-night cup of coffee with me?"

"Nope."

Tessa didn't realize her glib response would disappoint him so much. She placed her hand lightly on his shoulder.

"I would like to have a cup of hot cider or cocoa with you, instead?" she offered, smiling warmly.

"Not a big coffee fan?" He responded now with the light banter she was hoping for.

"Oh no, I love coffee, but I'm not typically in the mood for it so close to midnight. Another thing – nowhere around here other than the Waffle House is open, but I live in walking distance. Would you like to come over and hang out?" she asked.

"That'd be great. I'm not due back for shooting until tomorrow. It will be nice to just relax a bit with such a lovely woman."

Nate's ease at spouting kind words both fascinated and infuriated Tessa. It felt amazing to hear such great compliments, but it also made her just a little uncomfortable.

"I'm sure your order is up. I'll bring it right out." She literally bolted for the kitchen before he had a chance to surprise her with anything else.

Swinging through the kitchen doors, she nearly knocked down the rest of the wait staff – all of them finished with their shifts and simply hanging around to find out more about Nate Wilder.

She pushed through them, trying to keep as much information as possible to herself. The last thing Tessa wanted was more attention in regards to her relationships. Not that there was any sort of relationship at this moment with Nate, but it seemed like that could, despite her thinking the idea was completely out of left field, actually be a possibility in the very near future.

Chapter 2

"*What am I doing?*" The question kept repeating itself over and over in her head as she climbed into the sleek black sports car Nate was driving while in town. Tessa had told him repeatedly that she could just walk home – she only lived a half a mile from the town square – but Nate insisted on driving her home. She did see his point that it wouldn't seem right for him to drive over while she walked in the chilly February night, but it meant that he had to wait while she finished up at The Grille, which definitely caused more than a few suspicious looks from the other servers and kitchen staff.

Although she would be peppered with more than a million questions when she arrived for her shift tomorrow, Tessa decided she wasn't going to worry about it anymore. This incredibly attractive man, who made her laugh and had a healthy dose of endearing charm, wanted to hang out with her, and she owed it to the both of them to see if sparks were going to fly.

"So where do we go from here?" Nate asked after he'd held the door for her, and had taken his own place in the driver's seat.

"I guess we just hang out and see what happens, no pressure, you know?" Tessa replied, happy that some of the questions swirling inside of her head were able to be vocalized. Nate's bewildered face, however, did not give her any comfort.

"I meant, like, literally. Do I take a left or right?" he explained with a laugh. Tessa felt her cheeks grow warm with embarrassment. She'd totally just stuck her foot in her mouth.

"Pull out, take a left and then it's the second street on the right, fourth house on the right," she told him, and chose not to mention anything else about her slip-up.

Two minutes later, Tessa directed Nate to pull into the drive and head just past the large antebellum style home to where he parked in front of the carriage house apartment that Tessa called home.

She led Nate up the stairs and onto the tidy little porch complete with potted pansies and her great-grandmother's rocker. Just inside her front door was a small foyer that held a small bench and a coat rack and led into the rest of the apartment. Thankfully, the entire top floor was hers to call home.

"Welcome to my home. It isn't anything grand, but it's comfortable here and I love it," Tessa said as she clicked on a few lamps when they walked into her main living area. A slip-covered sofa and tufted wingback chair were her main furnishings, and the left wall held built-in bookshelves that flanked both sides of a stone fireplace. Just to the right, a galley kitchen and a small pedestal table claimed most of the space.

A tiny hall held two doors, one to her bedroom and the other to the only bathroom.

"If you'll excuse me for just a moment, I'd really like to change," Tessa said as she hung her bag on the hook in the foyer.

"Of course, take your time," Nate told her, taking a seat on the sofa. He definitely didn't seem to have any problem making himself at home.

Tessa scurried to her bedroom and opened the closet door, not sure what in the world to wear. She couldn't pull out a stunning ensemble – that definitely wouldn't fit the situation, but she also didn't want to look like a total bum in a pair of sweatpants. After a couple of moments, she finally settled on a pair of patterned leggings and an ivory sweatshirt tunic with the words, "All that glitters is gold," written in sparkly lettering across the chest.

"What would you like to drink?" Tessa asked as she breezed back into the living area. "I have hot tea, apple cider, I do have coffee if you really want some, and there's a bottle of red wine I've been saving for a special occasion," she rattled off all that her kitchen had to offer.

"Oh, I'm definitely thinking the wine," he said with a confirming nod.

"Good, that's what I was hoping you would say," she said with a smile.

After she'd poured them each a glass, she brought it over to the sofa and sat down close, but not too close, to Nate. As she handed Nate his glass, he leaned it back to her direction as if to toast her and with a tender smile softening his rugged features, he said, "To you, Tessa, and to what I hope will be the beginning of something wonderful."

Tessa clinked her glass against Nate's, and gazed sweetly into his eyes. She was mesmerized. This wasn't turning into the fun and casual thing she thought she had signed up for – it was much more intense. Things were taking a romantic turn swiftly, and although she was determined not to fall too quickly for Nate, as she sat there beside him on her sofa, all of her reasonable defenses weren't working.

Before she completely got ahead of herself, Tessa cast her eyes down, and took a sip from the glass in her hand. "I'm really glad you're here, Nate," she told him, even if she didn't trust herself to look at him at the moment. Just the nearness of him was driving her crazy, and if she were to lock eyes with him again, Tessa knew that she would be a goner.

"Right now, there isn't a place in the world that I'd rather be," he murmured softly. Nate's words resonated deeply within Tessa, and she decided to venture another look into his beautiful eyes.

Somehow, subconsciously they had edged closer together and were now sitting mere inches apart, and their legs were brushing against one another. When Tessa finally allowed herself to glance up, she was staring directly into Nate's eyes, and what she found in their depths gave every indication that he was as smitten as she was.

"Nate, you have no idea what you are doing to me," she said, shaking her head, hoping the movement would shake off the heady spell he was putting her under.

"It's like I can't help myself. I'm drawn to you like a moth to a flame," Nate said, softly but frankly. Tessa understood what he meant – she was feeling the exact same way. But, it didn't change the fact that she was determined to stay strong in her resolve not to tumble into bed with him tonight.

"I think I need to move around or something," she said, setting her glass on the side table and stretching. Nate followed suit, and his face lit up with an idea. "Let's dance," he said, standing up and reaching out a hand to help her up from the sofa.

Tessa couldn't believe this night was taking yet another completely surreal turn. In what world did a movie star ask to dance with you in your living room after meeting you randomly at the restaurant where you waitress? Surreal. Totally surreal. With a toss of her ponytail over her shoulder, she decided to just go with it, and live in the incredibly crazy moment.

"Hold on just a second, let me find a good song," Tessa said as he helped her up. She grabbed her phone, hit a play list she'd already saved, and stuck it into the docking station.

Nate's face showed his surprise as the first few notes filled the air. "Really, Tessa?" he asked, arching an eyebrow.

"Really," Tessa winked at him as a classic country song filled the air.

"I seriously don't even know how one would go about attempting to dance to this," he said as he extended his hand.

"Well, let's just make it up as we go," she smiled, and he pulled her into his embrace. It definitely wasn't a typical dance song – it was sort of slow with the singer crooning about his lonesome heart, but it wasn't rhythmical in any way, shape or form. After a few swirls around the room, they both burst out laughing.

"Okay, okay, you're right, it isn't working," she admitted with an amused roll of her eyes. She flipped through the songs, settling on a cover version of "Problem" by Noah Guthrie. As the first notes began to fill the room, she took the hand Nate was extending to her and they began to move around the room to the sultry song.

"I really like this song," Nate murmured, his lips close to her ear.

"Yes, it's very good," Tessa replied, closing her eyes and drinking in the nearness of Nate and the beautiful lyrics. Maybe she was crazy, opening her heart and feeling so much emotion for someone she'd known for only a few hours, but the tender way Nate's hands securely held her waist and the intimate embrace they now shared was like a healing balm. All of the hurt and pain Davis had inflicted was melting away. Even if the reprieve was temporary, Tessa welcomed it wholeheartedly. She needed this.

As the song ended and another soft, acoustic ballad filled the air, Tessa laid her head against Nate's shoulder and he rubbed his hands slowly up and down her back. He exuded a protective nature that literally made every inch of her tingle with desire for him. Tessa smiled into his shirt, thinking how ironic it was that the fact that he wasn't coming on to her made her wish that he would do just that.

A moment later, as they continued to slowly move to the music, Nate leaned down and kissed the top of her head. Tessa lifted her cheek from his shoulder, stared into his lovely deep blue eyes, and she knew it was about to happen. The moment was there – that mesmerizing web that seemed to be woven before an epic kiss took place.

Nate leaned down and placed his lips softly against hers. Tessa welcomed his kiss as she molded her lips to his. The kiss started slowly and gently. It was obvious that they were each afraid of scaring away the other and were both holding back as the intensity continued to grow. But, holding back actually caused the slow kiss to smolder into something incredibly hot.

Neither pulled away, instead they just stayed still in the perfect moment, locked in one another's arms, lips melting together in a sizzling kiss that was slowly but surely turning into a blazing fire. The intensity heightened, and the sweetness gave way to eager desire. Nate pulled her more tightly against him and Tessa ran one of her hands into the slight bit of curl at the nape of his neck.

This moment was delicious, and she didn't want it to ever end. Nate pulled his lips away from hers to place them against her ear. "You're beautiful," he whispered before reclaiming her lips with his.

An unbidden tear slipped down Tessa's cheek, and she didn't care. She hadn't ever felt this...cherished. When Nate caressed her face and felt the dampness of her cheek, he pulled back and studied her face.

"What's wrong, Tessa?" he asked, putting his forehead against hers.

"Not a single thing. I just didn't expect...this."

"Neither did I. I expected fun, and I expected attraction, but not this level of intensity – this deep, almost raw feeling."

"Exactly. It's almost scary."

"Don't be scared. Let's just dial it back a bit," he said, wiping away her tear. Tessa nodded. Nate let go of her, took her hand in his and led her to the sofa.

"Why don't we just talk?" he suggested.

"I'd like that a lot," Tessa replied, snuggling up against his side as he put his arm around her.

For the next several hours they talked, and talked, and talked. They talked about things they loved, God, family, their childhood fears, their past relationships, their favorite foods – literally nothing was kept off of the table. And as the sun began to change from the deepest of blacks to a fuzzy shade of just-before-dawn gray, Tessa couldn't hold her eyes open any longer, and she drifted off to sleep with her head in Nate's lap and a smile on her face as he played with tendrils of her hair.

The bright, midday sun was warm on her face when she began to stir from her very uncomfortable position on the sofa. Tessa sat up and stretched her arms and yawned as the memories of the night before flooded her thoughts. It had been one of the best nights of her life – she'd never opened up like that with a guy, not even Davis.

She looked around the room. Where was Nate?

"Nate?" she called out tentatively. No one answered. *Hmm*, she thought. Had he just left without even saying goodbye? Tessa got up and headed to the kitchen, desperate for coffee and more than a little worried that Nate had just decided to head out without saying anything.

She noticed the piece of paper on the counter immediately. Picking it up, she read the note Nate had left her.

Tessa,

I was called to the set. Sorry I left without telling you, but you were sleeping so soundly, I didn't want to wake you. I can't wait to see you again – I know you are working tonight, but do you want to hang out again after? Text me and let me know.

I miss you already.

Nate

The simple sweetness of his words warmed her heart. Of course she wanted to see him again tonight! And every night! She hung the note on the fridge, and hurried to get the coffee maker going. Tessa had slept so late that she didn't have too much time to get anything accomplished before she needed to get ready for work.

When a steaming cup was finally in her hand, she headed to the small office area she'd carved out in her tiny apartment. Whenever she had free time, she tried to be here, working on her passion. It was her goal to write a book and have it published. Not self-published, but big-deal, major publishing house published.

And at the moment, as her heart was still soaring from her romantic evening with Nate, she was feeling unbelievably inspired. Her fingers flew quickly across the keyboard as words poured out of her.

An hour later, she'd written a decent chapter. Tessa was quite pleased with herself, especially since she'd only managed to squeeze out a paragraph or two that was of any worth since her breakup with Davis. Tessa smiled to herself, surprised at how much could change overnight. Nate was turning out to be the perfect distraction she'd needed to forget about all of the heartache she'd been enduring over the past few weeks.

Finished with her coffee and her writing, Tessa got dressed for work, taking a little more time than usual. She wanted to look her best when she met up with Nate later. It was so nice to finally have something to genuinely look forward to, and she relished the wonderful feeling.

Big Love in a Small Town

***

"So what were you up to last night?" Ansley Madison asked Nate as they waited to film another outdoor scene near Clearhill's town square.

"Nothing, just grabbed dinner," Nate replied, not wanting to share details about what he had been doing afterward. Meeting Tessa was an unexpected experience, and he wanted to keep it to himself. As soon as someone found out, it would be all over the internet and magazine covers. Tessa would probably bolt like a frightened deer if that happened.

"You're an old fuddy-dud, you know that, right? You should have gone into Atlanta with us last night," Ansley said.

"Call me what you want. I'm not really into the whole club scene – you know that," Nate pointed out. He and Ansley had known each other for a while, and occasionally tabloids tried to stir up gossip about them dating, but they had always and would always be just friends.

"I know. I know. Lord help you, Hollywood's heartthrob, hanging out in his hotel room watching Netflix – I'm sure they won't be able to keep the shelves full when that story breaks," Ansley said sarcastically, and Nate rolled his eyes.

"Well, I'd prefer if they never wrote anything about me at all, but I know it's a necessary evil."

Big Love in a Small Town

"You're right, it is. I think it's kind of funny – like, what outrageous rumor can they come up with this week?" Ansley laughed, and continued laughing as she made her way to the set where they were waiting for her.

After she left, Nate checked the messages on his phone and his heart leapt a little in his chest when he saw that he had one from Tessa.

"Your note was sweet. Meet me at The Grille at closing?" the message read.

Nate quickly typed back, "Sounds good. Can't wait until then." And he really couldn't.

The day dragged on endlessly with lots of waiting around on his and the other cast members' parts. During a particularly long wait between set changes, he took a much needed nap in his trailer. After all, it had been past sunrise this morning when he dozed off on Tessa's couch, and he had gotten a call to arrive in hair and makeup by eight.

Finally, filming wrapped and Nate headed to his no-frills hotel room. Clearhill only had three hotels and they were all pretty basic accommodations. They definitely wouldn't be categorized as luxurious, that's for sure. Honestly, Nate much preferred Tessa's cozy little apartment, but at least his temporary home was clean and not too far from the filming site.

Now, what was he going to do to fill the next three hours while he waited for Tessa's shift to end? With a sigh, he scrounged around in his leather messenger bag – the one that went on every trip with him – for the current historical biography he was reading. He smiled to himself, thinking how many of his adoring fans would keel over in confusion when they found out that he spent his spare time reading biographies and not hanging out at bars and trying to hook up with other stars.

A couple of hours later, he closed the book about Theodore Roosevelt, and hopped in the shower. Afterward, while getting dressed in jeans and a black V-neck T-shirt, Nate couldn't believe that he actually felt nervous. What was going on? He was a confident guy, and usually, women were jumping over one another for the chance to be with him. Not that he took advantage of that – he actually tried really hard to date women that didn't seem star-struck. But Tessa, Tessa was a different story entirely.

Tessa stirred feelings in him that he didn't even realize he was capable of having. She was spontaneous, honest, gorgeous, and made him laugh constantly. There was a frankness about her, despite her overall gentle demeanor, that fascinated him, and he was genuinely afraid, for the first time in forever, that he might scare her off with this crazy lifestyle that he lived.

Big Love in a Small Town

***

Tessa hurried to change in the bathroom at The Grille before Nate arrived. She was so excited to get to see him again, and she'd been so good about not telling anyone about it.

Although Nate hadn't asked her to keep their seeing one another a secret, she figured the guy always had some sleazy tabloid reporters skulking around, just waiting for some scrap of information that they could turn into a crazy story. Tessa didn't want to make a bigger deal about his celebrity status than it already was, so she'd simply kept it to herself that Nate had spent the night at her home and that he was coming over again tonight.

The attention wouldn't necessarily bother her, but after spending so much time with Nate last night, she knew that he loved acting and everything about the film industry, but he'd recently been burned by a few crazy rumors. He was now making a point to keep a minimal spot in the public eye, and that was fine with her.

Of course, she thought it was cool that she was seeing someone so completely adored by millions of people – who wouldn't find that fascinating? But at the same time, Tessa was going to make a specific point not to get hung up on celebrity status.

Freshly changed into jeans and a deep-blue sweater, Tessa said hurried goodbyes to everyone and headed out of the back kitchen door and into the chilly night. She picked up the quickest pace she could handle in her ankle boots, and jogged to Nate's waiting car. A quick thrill of excitement at getting to see him again ran down her spine.

"Hello there," she said as she tossed her bag onto the tiny back seat.

"Hello, Tessa," Nate smiled at her before leaning over to give her a kiss on her cheek.

"What do we have planned for the evening? Would you like to go back to my place again?" Tessa hoped he didn't think her too forward, but there just weren't that many options for things to do in Clearhill, and her place was private and away from prying eyes.

"That's fine with me. I honestly don't care what we do – I just enjoy spending time with you," he told her as he backed the car out of the parking spot. Tessa smiled at his words – he'd said them so matter-of-factly.

As they headed down the street, Tessa placed her hand in his as it rested casually on the center console. With her fingers laced between his, Nate gave her hand a squeeze. Tessa breathed in the moment of contentment. She didn't know where this was headed, but she was determined to continue to live in the moment and enjoy each second. She refused to over-analyze or worry about what would happen in the future – she was going to live in the right now.

Once they had arrived at her apartment and shed their coats, Tessa started a pot of coffee.

"I thought you didn't like to drink coffee at midnight," Nate remarked.

"Typically, no, I don't, but I'm a bit sleepy from staying up so late last night, and I don't want to pass out on the sofa," she said with a wink. "Would you like some?"

"I never turn down coffee. Can I help you with anything?"

"Nah, I've got it." She reached into one of the cabinets and pulled out a couple of cups. When she set them on the counter and whirled around to pull the creamer out of the refrigerator, she was met with Nate standing right there – so close that she nearly ran into him. She hadn't noticed his quiet approach. She'd been completely focused on getting coffee.

"Wh–What are y–" the question didn't make it out of her mouth as his lips captured hers and his hands encircled her waist. Taken by complete surprise, Tessa stood frozen for a fraction of a second before she figured out what was going on, and proceeded to wrap her arms around him while eagerly returning his fervent kiss.

The coffee maker beeped to alert them that it was finished brewing, but that was of no importance as several moments passed with them tangled in the hottest embrace she'd ever felt. Tessa was so wrapped up in Nate that she had no idea what existed outside of the two of them – a drawer knob was certainly making a nice indentation in the small of her back, but she didn't care. As Nate's lips moved on hers and his hands massaged up and down her back she began to crave more, and she wasn't about to pass up the opportunity for more tonight.

Tessa was nearly intoxicated as she gasped for breath between his kisses. She only had one thing on her mind when she broke away from him, and with desire in her eyes, huskily whispered, "Bedroom?"

As she waited for Nate to respond, she could tell, as he studied her, that he was searching for any reserve whatsoever on her part.

"I want this. I know you want this, too," she murmured, trying to wipe away Nate's doubt that she wasn't certain of her decision.

"Of course, I want you. We can slow down, though – there's no need to rush. It doesn't have to be tonight," he said, even as Tessa saw the smoldering desire in his eyes just before he leaned down and started kissing her neck.

Tessa ascertained that as much as Nate was saying he wanted to take things slowly, his actions were definitely proving otherwise. His kisses trailed down her neck and along the bit of collarbone Tessa's sweater had left exposed. When the stubble from his five o'clock shadow deliciously grazed against the tender skin there, shivers of excitement coursed through her body.

Now, Tessa decided that it was time she took matters into her own hands. Clearly, Nate was wrestling with what decision was the right one to make, so Tessa would simply decide for the both of them. She willed herself to pull away from his embrace, took him by the hand and slowly meandered into her dimly lit bedroom.

"Tessa, are you s—"

"Shh..." she interrupted him, placing her finger to his warm lips. Tessa took a step back and pulled her sweater over her head and began to unfasten the button on her jeans. Before she could finish, Nate tossed his own shirt over his head and pulled her into his arms.

She smoothed her hands over his perfectly defined chest, loving the way his skin felt hot against hers. Tessa tilted her head back and closed her eyes as his hands trailed softly down the sides of her waist before moving to the button she had been distracted from unfastening. Nate slowly unbuttoned her jeans and eased the zipper down, but didn't continue any further, which drove her mad.

Instead, he chose to slide his hands up her stomach and over her breasts, molding his palms against their soft peaks before sliding each of his thumbs into the frilly bra cups, pushing the material down and baring her skin. The underwire of her bra kept her breasts pushed up and together as Nate took one of her nipples into his mouth. As his tongue flicked against the sensitive flesh, Tessa let out a small moan of pleasure.

Nate took his time, kissing and caressing each of her breasts in turn. Tessa clung to his muscled back, arching towards him, trying to absorb all that she could as he continued to draw her so close to exploding with pleasure, but not allowing her to fully reach it yet.

He walked her backwards until her legs brushed against the bed, and gently tumbled them both down onto it, not letting go of Tessa in the process. Things quickly became more urgent as they helped one another out of the rest of their clothing.

When every inch of her bare skin was finally against every inch of Nate, Tessa felt like every nerve ending in her body was on exquisite edge. She hooked one of her smooth, silky legs over his taut ones. Nate ran a hand along the length of her thigh, trailing back up to her waist before sliding his fingertips over her hips and reaching between her thighs.

Tessa came alive at the sensation of Nate touching her intimately, and his lips found hers when her body tightened as intense pleasure began building deep within her. Just when she thought that there was no way possible that she could handle these feelings for a second longer, the pleasure was intensified when Nate moved over her body and found his way gently inside of her.

The moment it first happened was sweet and tender. The hot, pooling desire was there – but Tessa caught Nate's eyes at the instance their bodies became one, and they weren't glazed over with lust. Nate saw her, and she saw him. Intense adoration was in his eyes. Tessa was overwhelmed and she gasped as Nate moved within her. She wrapped her arms around him, pulling him tightly against her, and trying to take in all that her heart could hold.

Making love to Nate and experiencing such an emotional connection hadn't been part of the evening plans, and it was affecting every aspect of her being in a way that left her both scared and excited at the same time.

Nate brushed his hand against her cheek and Tessa let out a breathy sigh, arching her back as she gave in to the waves of pleasure raking over her body. If it was possible to capture perfect moments in time,

Tessa would have captured this one. She ran her fingers through his hair and smiled as Nate tensed over her when his own release came a couple of moments later.

Time slowly passed as they regained their composure, and Nate pulled her tightly against him, curling her long hair around his neck. Tessa grabbed the hem of her quilted coverlet and tossed it over their naked, intertwined bodies and fell into a blissful, sated sleep – a smile still on her peaceful face.

Chapter 3

"So you're telling me that you and Nate Wilder are just friends," Natalie stated, completely in disbelief as she and Tessa ate lunch together.

"Yes, that's what I'm telling you," Tessa fibbed, thinking about the amazing shower sex she had before work this morning. Sure, she'd only met Nate three weeks ago, but they spent every moment that they could together. If he wasn't on set, Nate was at her apartment. They simply could not get enough of one another.

In that short time, Tessa felt like she was constantly walking on clouds, and a permanent smile was affixed to the lips that Nate had kissed awake every morning for the past three weeks. Things between them were amazing, and beyond perfect. Not only was their physical chemistry like nothing Tessa had ever experienced before, but she also enjoyed just hanging out with Nate. They made each other laugh, they shared secrets with one another and pretty much existed in a perfect bubble that Tessa loathed leaving whenever she had to work or Nate had to film.

Tessa loved every moment of their time together and would have gladly shouted from the rooftops that she was dating a wonderful man, but they were trying to keep their fledgling relationship a secret, and it was proving to not be an easy task. Her recent and radical mood change from deep, dark melancholy to bright, shining euphoria was quite obvious to her circle of friends. She knew that she needed to finally tell them something, and saying that she had made a new "friend" in Nate Wilder seemed like a sufficient enough story to her.

"You know I don't believe you," Natalie stared at her from across the table. Tessa took a bite of her salad, refusing to budge any further on details, but couldn't help the slight slip of a smile at the mere mention of Nate's name.

"Are you really not going to eat, Nat?" Natalie was continuing to stare as her sandwich sat untouched on her plate. Tessa took another bite, hoping Natalie would follow suit. Their lunch break didn't last all day, after all.

"Not until you admit the truth to me."

"I don't have anything to admit."

"You are so full of it, Tess. Are you sleeping with him or what? Have you at least kissed? Come on! Tell me something that at least resembles the truth. I'm not buying the 'we're just friends' crap. I've known you forever, and all the signs are there that you are either getting it on, or you are about to be getting it on, with him."

Tessa felt her cheeks flush at her friend's frank words. She didn't like lying to Natalie, but at the same time, she didn't want Natalie's opinion on what was happening with Nate either. "You seriously aren't going to give up, are you? I can't believe you won't just drop it. If there was something to tell you, then I'd tell you."

"And I would totally believe you if you weren't acting like a lovesick teenager. I'd also believe you if this could be filed under normal circumstances, but Nate Wilder isn't normal circumstances. You are holding out on me and I know it. Just admit it – I promise I won't tell a soul."

They were at a stalemate. Tessa knew that Natalie was not going to stop pushing the issue, and Tessa wasn't about to spill the beans. The crazy whirlwind that she had been swept up in over the past few weeks with Nate was new and special, and Tessa thought if she wanted it to stay that way, she wouldn't be sharing the news with anyone anytime in the near future.

Tessa gave her a wink and pretended to lock her lips with an imaginary key and toss it over her shoulder before rummaging in her purse for her wallet. She figured that the little gesture should at least somewhat satisfy Natalie's rabid curiosity without Tessa actually having to say anything or go into details.

"I KNEW IT!" Natalie shouted before grabbing her sandwich off of her plate and taking a huge bite.

"You don't know anything! Hush!" Tessa defended, now regretting her momentary lapse in judgment. She shouldn't have given away anything.

"Sorry! Not another peep from me until you say something more. But for the record, I. Knew. It. The. End." Natalie winked at her and proceeded to finish her lunch without mentioning Nate's name again. Tessa rolled her eyes at her silly friend.

When they had parted ways, hurrying to get back to their respective offices, Tessa couldn't help but walk a little slower than she should as she passed by the set where Nate's movie was currently filming. She strained her neck to try and get at least a peek of him somewhere on the town's square. It was weird being so close to him, but at the same time, a whole world away.

Her phone vibrated in the pocket of her jacket. Pulling it out, she hurriedly read the text message she'd just received from Nate.

"I see you," it read. Tessa lifted her head up and looked all around in every direction. Where was he?

"Where are you?" she quickly typed back.

"To your left, waiting for the director. Surrounded by crew. You look so hot with your hair pulled back like that."

She looked in the direction he'd told her, her hand subconsciously patting the sleek ponytail he had just complimented. Although there were what felt like a hundred crew members in black T-shirts milling around, she finally spotted him standing in the middle of the crowd as someone tucked and fiddled with his clothing, and a stylist worked on his hair. He must have been waiting to officially film a scene, hence the need for the stylist's sole focus on him.

Nate caught her eye and gave her a sexy wink. She felt the blush on her cheeks and the heat spread inside of her as she recalled what they had been doing only a few hours ago.

Tessa sent him another message. "Will I see you later?"

She saw him look down to read the message, then he found her eyes and gave her that look, the look that caused her to shiver, and not from the chilly day, before replying, "I should be finished shooting by six. I'll head right over. I miss you."

Tessa smiled as she read his words and gave him a little wave before she semi-sprinted back to the newspaper office to avoid being late from lunch. A stack of assignments was waiting for her, but she didn't mind. She cheerfully settled in, knowing that keeping herself busy would make the time tick quickly by until she would be with Nate once more.

Big Love in a Small Town

***

Nate didn't care to take the time for official goodbyes when shooting finally wrapped for the day. He was beyond ready to be at Tessa's. All day, every day, all that he could think about was Tessa – her sweet, thoughtful ways, her beauty that would put anyone in Hollywood to shame. Tessa was the whole package, gorgeous both inside and out. And now that he had just been informed he would only be in town shooting for three more days, Nate didn't want to waste a single second longer than he had to being away from her.

He knew he had to tell her that he would be leaving soon, but it wouldn't be a problem for him to continue their relationship despite the long distance. Nate hated the idea of not seeing her every day, but there was no doubt in his mind that they could figure out a way to make this wonderful relationship work.

Nate raced up the stairs to her apartment, and Tessa opened the door before he even had a chance to knock.

"I was waiting for you," she explained, wrapping her arms around his neck as he scooped her up and kissed her. This was what he looked forward to the most whenever they were apart for any amount of time – the moment when they first connected again, the moment that felt like *home*. Tessa would wrap her arms around him, truly happy to see *him*, not Nate

Wilder, the actor or celebrity or whatever, but Nate Wilder, the regular guy that was head over heels for a beautiful girl with long, brown hair that smelled like apples.

"I love that you were waiting for me," he whispered against her neck, still holding her as he shut the door with his foot.

They wasted no time as they headed straight to her bedroom and spent the next few hours wrapped in each other's arms. Nate hadn't even realized how much time had actually passed as he traced along her side with his fingertips until he heard her stomach beginning to growl.

Looking over at the vintage alarm clock on her nightstand, he couldn't believe it was nearly eleven. "No wonder you're hungry! I'm starving myself! Time flies when you're having fun, you know," he murmured against her shoulder before kissing it. He would never get tired of kissing her.

"Well, what should we do for dinner?" Tessa asked.

"Whatever you want to do is fine with me."

"Waffle House?"

"Sure, why not?"

Tessa and Nate hopped out of bed and quickly dressed before heading out to the one restaurant in town that was open at that hour. It had actually become a regular thing over the past couple of weeks for them to dine at Waffle House. Mainly, because they were always in need of food at weird times and Waffle House was open twenty-four hours, but also because the cinnamon waffles tasted like heaven, and had quickly became his favorite thing about Clearhill after Tessa.

"I sure am going to miss these," Nate said absentmindedly as he took a bite of the scrumptious waffle. They were sitting in a booth – the only customers in Waffle House at this time of night. As soon as the words left his mouth, the look on Tessa's face made him immediately regret them.

Tessa held her fork frozen in midair and her face turned pale. "Why did you say that? Are you leaving soon?" she asked, trying to seem nonchalant, but her voice wavered.

Nate ran his hand through his hair, cursing himself for his slip of tongue. He wasn't mentally prepared for this conversation yet.

"I actually wanted to talk to you about that earlier, but we kind of got carried away..." he trailed off with a smile, trying to lighten the mood. Tessa, however, stared at him blankly. She was clearly not amused as she waited for him to continue.

"I was informed today that we should be finished shooting in three days." There, he said it.

"So you're leaving in three days?"

"Not necessarily – these things are never set in stone, it's just a rough estimate, and it's not like I have to leave the moment shooting is finished."

"So you are leaving in three days. Roughly." Tessa's deadpan face worried Nate. This did not bode well.

"Tessa, please don't think whatever it is that you're thinking. You and I both know that this isn't just a fly by the seat of your pants kind of fling. I truly care about you," he reasoned. The last thing he wanted to do was lay his cards out on the laminate table at the Waffle House, but he couldn't just sit there without making it clear how much she meant to him.

"Look, Nate, you really don't have to explain. I don't know what I was thinking. Of course, you have to finish shooting and of course, you have to go back to LA. Where you live," she said with a too-bright smile suddenly plastered on her face. It was as if Tessa had decided to detach and put on a mask, and he didn't like it at all. Why was she shutting down so abruptly?

"Tessa," he lowered his voice and looked intently into her eyes, "please don't do this. I can see and feel you shutting me out. I want you to know that…that I'm falling in love with you." He had wanted to tell her that in the right place at the right time, but seeing her slip through his fingers was causing him to pull out all the stops. It was the truth anyway.

She looked up when he admitted those words. Surely, Tessa must have known that this was the case. Wasn't it obvious to her that he couldn't get enough her? That seeing her smile made the most trying days on set absolutely worth it?

"What did you say?" she quietly asked.

"I said that I'm in love with you. I love you, Tessa," he repeated.

"That's what I thought you said. How could you do this, Nate?" her voice broke. Nate watched in horror as unbidden tears spilled down her cheeks. What was happening?

"Tessa, I don't understand. I'm telling you that I love you and you're mad at me. What am I missing?"

"There's no way you could be in love with me after just a few weeks. Clearly, I mean very little to you, and you are just saying anything and everything to make your last few days here pleasant before you move on to someone else. Just take me home," she said.

Nate could sense the moment she reined in her emotions and a frosty glaze encased her heart, protecting herself from him. How could things have gone so wrong and why did she insist that she knew how he felt about her more than he himself did? Now it was his turn to get mad.

"Fine, Tessa. I'll take you home, but I hope you get the chance to sit back and really think about what just happened. At what point did I ever give you any reason to doubt that I'm telling the truth? That I truly do love you, and think about you all the time and can't wait to just simply be in your presence?" he said with emphasis.

Before Tessa could respond, he jumped up to pay the check and then waited to hold the door open for her so that he could take her home. If she was going to be this way, he was going to give her the evening and the space to get over it.

He'd call her in the morning after she had time to process her feelings. Surely, she would come to realize that she was being hasty in assuming that his feelings were only for sport, and then they could move on and put this first little spat behind them.

***

Tessa knew it had been too good to be true. How many times had she repeated that mantra over and over to herself in the past couple of weeks? At least two hundred times, she figured.

She'd been up all night pacing her living room after Nate had dropped her off following the Waffle House debacle. It was better, she supposed, that it ended now anyway – before she really lost her head and fell completely, irrevocably, face forward in love with him. She would have been an absolute fool to do that, and she saw it now.

How dare he drop the L word after just a few weeks! She knew he was just using it as a last resort to make her less angry with him. Nate didn't have any idea that it would make her feel so...cheap and used. Maybe other girls before her thrilled at the idea of being told a celebrity was in love with them, and would easily get caught up in the whirlwind romance of it all. Not this girl, oh no.

Tessa had gotten to know, well, assumed that she'd gotten to know, the real Nate Wilder, and in real life, people didn't just go around pronouncing their love for someone after knowing them for just a few weeks.

Tessa figured that he must have filmed so many movies now that he was having a hard time figuring out what was acceptable in normal, everyday real life, and what was just the stuff made up for fairy tales and chick flicks.

How could he ruin what they had shared like this? Her heart was sad, and she felt empty inside. There was no way she was going to see Nate again and continue to put herself through this torture. After all, she'd only recently ended things with Davis. What happened with Nate just went to prove that she obviously wasn't ready to start dating again. She should have been better at guarding her heart.

Sure, Nate had sent her dozens of messages and had attempted to call several times already this morning, but Tessa ignored them and would continue to do so. Her heart couldn't afford to be broken any further, and talking to Nate would make the pain worse. Her heart had already been ravaged by Davis, and what little bit had begun to heal was now completely smashed into tiny pieces by Nate.

She poured herself one more cup of coffee before deciding to finally bite the bullet and get ready for work. Despite her inner turmoil and lack of sleep, she still had to go on with her life. As she showered and dressed, she thought about how thankful she was that she hadn't really told anyone about her and Nate. How embarrassing would it have been when he left her high and dry for another girl at the next filming location!

Natalie might have known a little bit about Nate from Tessa's hints, but that could all be smoothed over and chalked up to a misunderstanding. *Yes*, Tessa thought and nodded her head at her reflection in the mirror, *I've got this. A little heartbreak, I can handle it. Just keep it together, Tess, and it will all be over soon.*

Chapter 4

Two months later...

Tessa's fingers flew across the keyboard. She paused only for a sip of coffee before they took off again. Never, in all the years of attempting to write her own novel, had the words poured out of her as they had in the last couple of months. She was well on her way to being finished with the first draft, and at no point had it really felt like work.

She smiled at the screen, thinking about how much she'd accomplished in such a short time, and how very invested she was in her characters and the paths that their fictional lives were taking. The timer on the dryer buzzed, and Tessa begrudgingly stopped to handle the necessities of everyday life.

As she flew around her apartment, taking care of mindless chores and making sure her home was neat and tidy, Tessa's mind wandered to thoughts of Nate. Sure, it had been two months since they'd spoken, but that didn't change the fact that Tessa still thought about him every single day. What was he doing? Was he happy? Did he still think about her?

When Tessa and Nate had had their final confrontation before he'd left, Nate had sworn up and down that his feelings were true and honest, and that he never went around just telling people that he loved them. But Tessa knew that at that point in her life when the situation with Nate had happened, she had been too vulnerable and too broken to actually be a functioning part of a healthy relationship. The wounds from Davis had been too fresh. She hoped beyond all hope that Nate would come to understand that eventually, but she still wasn't in a place where she felt comfortable contacting him to apologize for her brash behavior.

Maybe one day, she mused as she pushed the vacuum across the black-and-white woven rug. Deep down inside, Tessa knew she had really messed things up by jumping to conclusions, but it had taken a long time for her to come to that realization, and now she was pretty sure it was too late.

Not only had she let a large lapse in time pass by, but the thought of seeing him again caused her to blush with embarrassment. She didn't think he would want to see her anyway. Not after what she had done.

Finished with her routine, she closed and locked the door to her apartment and trudged down the stairs, pausing at the landing to let out a little sigh of regret. Normally, in the beautiful Georgia sunshine, as the April blooms arched picturesquely over the sidewalks and streets, her walk to work was pure pleasure. But today was one of those days where she tended to dwell on her wrecked love life more so than other days. Today wasn't good.

Tessa kicked at the rocks as she walked down the graveled drive to the main street. She wasn't always like this. Some days were definitely better than others – especially when she had been so focused on her work and diving into the novel she'd been dying to write for ages. Some things were really good, and she should be much more thankful for those things.

Why can't I just forget him? I messed it all up, it's my fault. Not his. I blew it and I need to get over it. Thoughts of their weeks together filled her mind as she attempted to repeat that mantra, but no matter how many times she did, it just wouldn't stick.

The work day blended together into a monotonous line of editing and proofreading with no real excitement. Tessa found herself counting the minutes until it was time to leave. Most days, she did enjoy her job – it was what she had gone to school for, after all. Today just wasn't her day. She had figured that out way earlier.

Tomorrow is another day, she thought to herself. If it worked for Scarlett O'Hara, the most iconic of all Southern belles, to repeat those words, surely it would work for her.

The air was a bit crisp on the walk back home, and she rubbed her bare arms as she silently wished she hadn't forgotten her sweatshirt at home that morning. Tessa hoped that there wouldn't be any more cold snaps and that spring was finally here to stay, but there was no getting around the evening chill that would last for at least a few more weeks.

Caught up in her myriad thoughts, she didn't notice someone sitting at the bottom of her steps, waiting for her to return home.

"Hello, Tessa."

Surprise and shock left her paralyzed. He was the last person that she ever imagined would be waiting for her.

"Um, hi, Davis," she said with uncertainty when she willed herself to finally say something. Tessa would need more than a minute to process this.

"I know you weren't expecting me, and I'm sorry to just surprise you," Davis said, standing as she made her way towards the steps.

"What are you doing here?" she blurted out. His face registered surprise at her bluntness, but Davis rallied quickly.

"I made a few decisions, and I needed to see you. Can I come up? I'd really like to sit down and talk. Maybe we could go to dinner."

"I don't know...we haven't seen or talked to each other in months. Not since you up and left town...and me."

"Tess, please, let me talk to you. I'm here to explain, and beg for your forgiveness. Just give me a chance to do that."

Tessa weighed her options. On one hand, she was still beyond pissed at Davis and how he had handled things. She knew, whether he admitted it or not, that something had happened between him and Shauna.

But on the other hand, she was interested in what he had to say, and they did have a history together. She supposed she owed him at least the opportunity to explain himself and apologize.

"Fine. You can come up. You have twenty minutes and we aren't going to dinner," she told him as she stalked past him and headed up the steps.

Davis followed her up and stood way too close as she fumbled with the lock. Even though she was angry with him, he was still easy on the eyes, dressed in a black shirt and jeans, with his dark hair tousled from the wind. Tessa would have to have her guard up. Rolling her eyes as he rested his hand on the small of her back in a far too familiar way, Tessa was pretty sure the next twenty minutes wasn't going to add any improvement to her bad day.

Once they were inside and seated, with Davis on the sofa and Tessa in an armchair a comfortable distance away from him, Tessa decided it was best to get straight to the point.

"Okay, Davis. What do you want to talk about?"

"Tess, I made a huge mistake breaking up with you, and I am so, so sorry. You were, and always will be, the best thing that has ever happened to me. Please forgive me."

Tessa raised an eyebrow. Obviously, Davis wasn't mincing words tonight.

"I forgive you, Davis. It's over, and there isn't any point in me holding onto any anger or sadness over what you did."

"That's great, Tess. I'm really glad to hear you say that."

"So how have things been going in Nashville?"

"Really good. We've been playing a lot of local bars and stuff, and we have a meeting next week with a record label. Things are looking awesome."

"How's Shauna?" Tessa couldn't help herself, and seeing Davis get slightly flushed only cemented what she'd already suspected.

"Shauna is...Shauna."

"What is that supposed to mean? You do know that I'm a pretty smart girl, right? Did you really think that I didn't see what was happening? What your real reason for breaking up with me was? I'm not stupid."

"No, Tess. Nothing happened before our breakup. I swear. But I'll admit, we did sort of date for a few weeks, but it ended up being a terrible idea. We are much better off as friends."

"Do you promise nothing happened before we broke up?"

"Cross my heart. I would never do that to you again after you took me back all those years ago. I learned my lesson. I only broke up with you because I was moving, and I knew the long-distance thing would be way too much of a strain on the both of us."

"I don't think it was fair that you made that decision on your own. It hurt, Davis."

"I know it did, and I'm really sorry." Davis rose from his place on the sofa and crossed the room to where Tessa was sitting.

Tessa stared at him in confusion. What did he think he was doing? To her surprise, he knelt in front of her and bowed his head against her knee. The gesture nearly broke her heart.

"I know that I don't deserve your forgiveness or another chance, but I will work every day trying to make it up to you. Tessa, the past few months without you in my life made me realize that I can't live without you," he continued. A tear slipped from Tessa's eye at the words he was saying, his voice thick with emotion.

"Davis," she tilted his chin up to look at her, "I can't do this again. I'm just now at the point where I can live again. You wrecked me."

"Tessa, I promise to be the man that you deserve. I love you – you are for me. No one else will ever do for me, and I know it."

"But you live in Nashville. You said yourself that we couldn't make a long-distance thing work," she pointed out.

"Move to Nashville. Tessa, it's amazing there – full of creativity and a vibrancy that you wouldn't believe. You and your writing would thrive there."

"Are you kidding me? Pick up and move to Nashville on a whim?" Tessa's jaw literally dropped as she stared at Davis incredulously.

"It's not a whim – we have so many years of history. You know me, Tess. Better than I probably know myself. And, I don't expect you to make this decision tonight. I just couldn't let the opportunity for happiness pass us by. Are you sure you don't want to go to dinner?"

"No, thank you. I need to sit and process my thoughts about all of this. Alone." Tessa was completely shell-shocked. This was what she had wanted all along. Months ago, she had longed for this very moment, and hoped that Davis would come to his senses. But in this moment, the only person she could think about was Nate. Thoughts of their slow dance in her living room, sweet kisses, and a million other memories flooded her mind as Davis eyed her.

The passion that she had shared with Nate made every moment of her years with Davis seem as if her world had been black-and-white. With Nate, she'd felt like she had been alive with vibrant color.

She showed Davis out, letting him hug her and allowing a small peck of a kiss. She really needed to sort all of this out, and she didn't really have anyone with whom she could truly discuss it.

Natalie never knew about what really happened with Nate, and was definitely not a fan of Davis. She would be way too biased to give a good opinion on what Tessa should do. Her friends at The Grille weren't close enough to share this huge life crisis with and expect a quality response.

Tessa wouldn't even have a moment's hesitation on what to do if it wasn't for Davis' heartfelt plea. She could literally feel the raw emotion as he had knelt in front of her. How could she not be moved by that?

Maybe she should give him another chance. She'd already decided she had to close the door on Nate, and she did have a long history with Davis to consider. Of course, they'd had their issues, but all in all, he'd generally treated her right and always been there for her.

They had basically grown up together, and in that, they'd both made mistakes and grown from them. Everything that had gone wrong between them hadn't been totally Davis' fault. She knew there were certain things for which she had been to blame.

With a frustrated groan, Tessa poured herself a glass of wine and sat before her computer. It was best to channel all of her frustration and emotion into her characters. This situation would make for some really good writing. She'd think about what to do in the morning after a good night's sleep. But for now, she was going to take full advantage of the emotions that would pour into the written word.

Chapter 5

The next morning, Tessa woke from a troubled sleep, still unsure how to handle the situation with Davis. She'd continued to write well past midnight, and despite her determination not to think about Davis' plea until the morning, she had laid awake for hours, tossing and turning as she replayed their conversation in her mind.

Should she give him another chance? Did he seriously want her to move to Nashville? And what about Nate? The man that, no matter how hard she tried, she just couldn't fully remove from her heart or her mind.

Tessa tried to push past the thoughts of Nate. That ship had sailed, and she couldn't base this decision on anything that had to do with him. Hadn't she hoped and wished for Davis to do exactly what he was doing now? Begging for forgiveness and wanting to sweep her away to live happily ever after was actually even more wonderful than her romantic heart had ever hoped for.

But why wasn't she more excited about it? Why hadn't she thrilled at his words and jumped into his arms immediately?

Tessa rose from her still warm bed and shuffled to the shower. Today was going to be interesting. With little sleep, tons of work to do, a shift at The Grille and Davis complicating everything, she wasn't necessarily sure she was ready for it.

When she arrived at work an hour later, a dozen creamy white roses in a beautiful vase were taking up a nice size portion of her desk. Tessa smiled – Davis sure was going all out in his attempt to rekindle their love.

She put her things down and poked around the lovely, expensive bouquet until she found the gold embossed card. It read:

Not one day has passed that you haven't been on my mind. You have my heart.

Tessa pressed the unsigned note against her chest. What a sweet, thoughtful gesture! Maybe she could give Davis another chance after all. She leaned down and inhaled the sweet, heady scent of the roses. There was definitely something to be said about roses and romance.

She pulled her phone from her pocket, but decided against texting Davis to tell him thank you. It would be better to say the words in person. Tessa took a seat at her desk, her mood boosted by the lovely bouquet that would keep her company today.

As the work day came to a close, Tessa texted Davis a quick message asking him to come over to her house for coffee in a little while. He responded almost immediately that he would be there, and was excited to see her. Feelings of nostalgia washed over her as she recalled all of the wonderful times she and Davis had shared.

She frowned a little as a vision of slow dancing in her living room with Nate popped into her head. She was trying to remember the past with Davis. With a sigh, she feared it was inevitable. Tessa would never be able to put her short fling with Nate behind her.

If she was honest with herself, she'd felt more passion in those few weeks with Nate than the entire time she'd been with Davis. She just couldn't make that a deciding factor in whether or not she was going to try with Davis again. After all, Nate was a gorgeous celebrity. Who wouldn't have passion that surpassed all others with someone like that?

Memories flooded her mind, but not of Davis. Unbidden thoughts of kisses and candlelight, waffles and incognito set visits made her ache for Nate. This was so unfair! She had Davis holding his heart out in his hands, and all she wanted was Nate. Plain and simple.

Oh well, Tessa. You had better just go on and get over that really quick. Don't miss out on what's right in front of you, she thought to herself.

On the walk home, she didn't rush as usual. Instead, Tessa spent some time in reflection, thinking about the decision she had to make. By the time she'd reached her apartment, she knew what she was going to do.

***

When Davis rang her doorbell a couple of hours later, Tessa opened the door and beamed happily at him.

"Hello, Davis," she greeted him warmly. His eyebrows rose in surprise.

"Hi there, Tessa," he replied as he leaned in to give her a hug and a lingering kiss on the cheek.

"Do you want something to drink?" she asked, leading him inside.

"What are my options?"

"I have wine, tea and coffee."

"Tea is fine – as long as it's sweet," he said, winking.

"Of course it's sweet, we're in the South," she said with a playful pat on his arm. She'd forgotten how easily conversation flowed for them.

Davis took a seat on the sofa while Tessa poured glasses of sweet tea.

"Tessa, I think things are looking amazing for our future in Nashville. You are the epitome of a Southern belle, who happens to be an incredibly talented writer, and you know what I can do with a guitar. We'll be the perfect songwriting pair," he told her when she'd sat down beside him.

Tessa nearly spit out the tea she'd just sipped.

"Songwriting? Davis, I've never written a song. Ever. You know I don't write songs."

"Why can't you? They're a lot shorter than what you normally write."

"Are you kidding me? There's a certain musicality and rhythm that's needed to write songs. I wish I had that, but I don't."

"Well, maybe with practice, it'll come. Never mind that, let me just tell you how glad I am that you asked me over tonight," he said, putting his arm around Tessa and scooting her closer to him.

"I thought I owed it to the two of us, and our history, to attempt reconciling, but I've got to be honest – I'm not ready to say, 'Hey, my bags are packed,' however, I am willing to try the long-distance thing," she explained. Tessa didn't want to beat around the bush any longer than necessary. She figured it was best to go ahead and shoot straight with Davis.

"Tessa, you know how I feel about long-distance relationships. They never end well. But, I want to be with you. What's keeping you here?" Davis wasn't happy. His brow was furrowed and he wore a pouty expression.

"This is my hometown. It's familiar. I know people. And to be clear, I never said I wouldn't move. If you would have asked me to go with you when you originally left, I would have gone and never looked back, but you didn't.

"I think we need to see where this goes – I'm not sure if we even feel the same way about each other, and I'm not agreeing to move anywhere without being absolutely certain that you're in it for the long haul."

"I can't believe you don't think I'm willing to make a long-term commitment to you. Seven years, Tessa! We were together seven years!" Davis said heatedly.

"I know that, Davis. But in those seven years, you cheated on me twice and just two months ago, you broke up with me and moved in with your band, which included a very hot girl. So don't go there and try to play that card," Tessa said, her own cheeks flaming.

Davis inhaled sharply as he closed his eyes. "Okay, you're right. Maybe I'm rushing things. I guess I figured I know now what it's like to be without you, and I don't ever want to go through that again."

Tessa put her hand on top of his. "That's very sweet. I appreciate your honesty – it means more than anything else. But, I'm still not moving to Nashville right now."

"Okay, I understand. We can try the long-distance thing and see what happens," he said with a reluctant but willing smile.

Tessa smiled in response. It was a start.

Davis leaned in to kiss her and Tessa tilted her chin to meet his lips. The kiss was nice and familiar, but it wasn't anything like the hot sparks and burning fire she felt every time Nate kissed her.

Ugh! Get a grip, girl! Stop thinking about Nate. Just stop it! She wasn't sure whether she would ever be able to get Nate out of her mind. How could such a short, little fling leave such an enduring impact on her? However, even if it was frustrating, it did settle one order of business.

"Davis, I'm sorry," Tessa whispered, pushing away from him.

"Sorry for what?" he asked, confused.

She didn't know why she was so compelled to do what she was about to do. Wasn't this exactly what she'd thought she'd wanted? For Davis to come waltzing back into her life, desperate for her, proclaiming his undying affection for her and her alone?

"I'm sorry, but this isn't going to work. I just don't feel the same way about you anymore," she blurted out before she lost courage.

"What? Are you joking right now? If you are, I don't think it's very funny."

"No, I'm serious. My feelings have changed. I'm sorry I led you on the past couple of days, but I was just trying to sort everything out. I've come to realize that we're both different people that lead different lives."

"But, we've got such a history–"

"Just stop right there," she interrupted him, "I know we have a history, and you will always be a part of my story, but our history is just that – history. You only think that you want to be with me because I'm familiar. You know me and it's a comfortable fit. But really think about it, Davis. If we truly were meant to be, would it have been so easy for you to cheat on me? Or leave me and go to Nashville?"

Davis was silent for a moment, contemplating her words. Tessa waited for him to respond with something – anything.

"As much as I hate to admit it, you've got a point. Although it's a point that makes me feel pretty shitty. But don't forget, Tess – you're just as much a part of my story as I'm a part of yours. I'll always love you, and you'll always have a part of my heart," he finally said. His voice rang true with emotion.

Tessa reached over and took his hand. "Right back at you, Davis. I will always love you, too," she replied, holding back tears. It was the bittersweet, official end of Davis and Tessa. Although it was the right thing for both of them, it was still the heartbreaking end of an era.

"Friends?" he asked her.

"Always," she replied.

After a long, unwavering embrace, Tessa showed Davis out for the very last time. "Oh, I forgot to tell you thank you for the lovely bouquet," she said at the door.

"And I would say 'you're welcome' if I had sent you flowers. You must have another admirer, Tess," he replied with a shrug.

At her confused look, with a hint of sadness, he added, "Whoever he is, he's one lucky guy if you decide to give him a chance. Hopefully he won't blow it like I did."

They lingered there for a moment longer, and when she said her last goodnight and closed the door behind him, Tessa leaned back against the heavy wood, letting the tears she'd bravely held back finally fall in abandon.

***

With the dawning of a new day came fresh perspective. As painful as it had been to let go of Davis, at last she felt free to move on with her future.

And she hoped her future would include a certain someone that had captivated her thoughts for months now.

Davis hadn't sent Tessa flowers. Which meant there was only one other person who would have sent them. Someone who must not be holding her ridiculous behavior against her as she'd assumed.

Tessa floated around her bedroom as she prepared for the day. She'd never felt so light. It was as if the world was aglow once more after being so very dark for far too long.

She hummed as she walked with a spring in her step to work. Maybe it was just her, but it seemed as if the air smelled sweeter, the sunshine was brighter than usual, and the blooms and flowers were more vivid. Tessa drank in the beauty of her little town and all of its Southern charm. No wonder so many studios liked to film there. The whole area was scenic perfection.

As the work day rolled along, Tessa's mind was on what step she should take next. Was she going to contact Nate? How would she do it? A phone call? A sentimental letter? Definitely not a text…

In the midst of writing a long editorial, she shouted out, "Of course!" before hunkering back down within the safe walls of her cubicle as her coworkers stared, trying to determine whether or not she needed medication.

She would go to Los Angeles and talk to him in person. Why hadn't she thought of it before? She had all of Nate's contact information, so she knew right where to go. Anything less just wouldn't suit the heartfelt message she needed to convey.

In between editing and writing, Tessa checked various websites for upcoming flights. When she spotted one that left a week from today at a great price, she snagged it, and before she left for the day, she arranged to take time away from work.

It hadn't been a problem since she never took time off. Mr. Hart was actually glad to hear that she was taking a vacation.

"It's high time you did something just for you, Tessa. You enjoy yourself, and tell us all about your trip when you get back," he'd told her with a patronizing pat on the head. Tessa rolled her eyes and smiled at the old man. He wouldn't ever see her as anything but a child. A dearly loved child, but a child nonetheless. She guessed that was part and parcel when your boss and his wife had taught your childhood Sunday school class.

Although she had kept Natalie out of the loop for most, well actually, all of her Nate issues, Tessa knew she needed her best friend as she prepared for her trip. Natalie's reply when Tessa texted her to come over that night was instantaneous and quite enthusiastic. Natalie had responded, "YYEESSS!!!!! It's been too long! I'm bringing the wine!!"

Tessa nearly jogged home, she was bursting with so much excitement and nervous energy. After all, she was flying across the country in a week to see the man of her (and probably a million other women's) dreams, and ask him for another chance. Who wouldn't be at least a little nervous?

When Natalie arrived, a bottle of pinot noir held in each hand, her brow was wrinkled with concern.

"What's wrong?" Tessa asked, taking one of the bottles and heading for the kitchen to crack it open.

"You look...crazed," Natalie said as she took in Tessa's appearance. Tessa was wearing a neon sports bra and black yoga pants, and her hair was pulled up in a disheveled bun.

"I finished a workout video just before you got here. Gotta get all of this," she gestured to her torso, "nice and tight."

"Well, this," Natalie waved the wine bottle, "isn't going to help out with that," she said, pointing to Tessa's already lean figure.

Tessa shrugged her shoulders. "I earned the wine. That workout kicked my butt." She finished opening the bottle, and poured them each a glass.

"So, tell me what's been going on," Natalie said, cutting right to the chase once they'd gotten comfortable.

"Davis came to see me."

Natalie nearly spit out the sip of wine she'd just taken. "For the love of all that is good, tell me you are not getting back together with him, Tessa."

"No, we aren't getting back together. We officially ended things once and for all, and we are both good with that. It was the closure I needed."

"I'm proud of you two, but I've got to admit, I'm also confused. I would've expected you to be in a way less chipper mood about it."

"I'm in such a good mood because I finally realized something wonderful."

"I'm waiting! Spit it out already!"

"I'm in love with Nate Wilder."

Tessa watched as Natalie eyed her. Doubt and concern crossed over her friend's face.

"Honey, he's a movie star. Half the population is in love with him."

"Yes, I know that. Let me back up and give you the whole story. Remember when they were filming here a few months ago?"

Tessa filled Natalie in on every tiny detail of what had happened with Nate so that Natalie would be able to give her a good perspective on whether or not she was making a wise decision.

"Tessa, I could smack you for giving him the brush-off like that! He obviously cared about you!" Natalie said when Tessa had finished her story.

"I know, I know, I could smack me too. But the truth is, I wasn't ready for another relationship at that point. I was still terribly hurt from being dumped. What happened with Nate was amazing and unexpected, but I still had a lot of Davis feelings to figure out."

Natalie rolled her eyes and poured them both another glass of wine. Tessa eagerly reached for hers. This conversation needed lots of wine.

"Do you think I'm crazy for going to see him?"

"No, not after what you just told me. It's important that you see him in person to explain how you feel."

"Okay, thank you. I needed someone other than myself to say that."

"I know you. I know that's what you needed, and if I thought it was a bad idea for you to go, I would totally tell you. And you know that."

"Oh, believe me, I know you are always straight-up honest with me. That's why I told you about everything. I needed to know the truth, and I knew you would give it to me. I'm just sorry it took so long for me to open up to you." Tessa took a long sip of her wine. The pinot noir was smooth, strong and just a little sweet.

"Well, here's to wooing the movie star," Natalie said, clinking her glass against Tessa's.

"There will be no wooing. The wooing already went down," Tessa said with a laugh. Her cheeks felt flushed from the wine and her laugh may have gone on just a little too long, but hey – sometimes you needed to get tipsy with your best friend and talk about boys. It was good for the soul.

"So when are you going?"

"I leave next Thursday."

"Wow. That's soon. You better get packing."

Chapter 6

Tessa struggled with her large suitcase, carry-on bag and purse as she made her way out of LAX and into the bright sunshine. Her flight had been smooth, and she'd arrived in Los Angeles in one piece. Now, if she could only manage to look graceful, like the other jet-setters scurrying around, as she maneuvered her luggage on the sidewalk to wait for a cab, she would be set.

Zinging with energy and excitement as anticipation of seeing Nate skyrocketed, Tessa's smile spread from ear to ear – even as she and the cabdriver wrestled her mountain of stuff into his trunk, and it continued to stay in place during the entire jerking, death-defying ride to the hotel where she'd booked a room. Nothing was going to take away from the sunshine her soul was radiating. Not even terrible cabdrivers.

She checked into her room and took a few moments to settle in and sort her thoughts. The room was simple yet elegant with fluffy white bedding and sleek furnishings. Tessa pulled her dresses and other clothing items that she didn't want wrinkled out of her suitcase and hung them inside the closet. She tucked her suitcase in there, too. The makeup bag, hair stuff and toiletries went into a neat row in the spacious white-tiled bathroom. When she was on vacation, she didn't like her room to feel cluttered with open bags and clothes strewn everywhere.

When Tessa felt that her room was in order and everything was put into place, she hopped into the shower. She didn't want to waste time. Her purpose here was to see Nate, and before she flew back to Georgia on Sunday, she wanted to spend as much time as possible with him.

An hour and a half later, Tessa's makeup was flawless, her tresses fell in long, bouncing curls down her back, her skin was moisturized and gave off the slightest scent of lavender, and she was dressed in a strapless, flowing black maxi dress. She was ready to see her love.

Pulling her phone out of her purse, she sent a quick text to Nate asking him what he was doing. She didn't want to contact him at all until she could see him, but finding him would be nearly impossible if she didn't. He didn't know she was in LA, of course, but if he told her where he was, she could figure out her next step. A moment later, he texted her back.

"Tessa! So good to hear from you! How are you? I'm eating an early dinner. We have a long night of shooting ahead."

"Oh, cool. I'm doing good. Where are you eating?" she texted back, a little disappointed that he wouldn't be free tonight. Nate probably was wondering why she

kept pressing on the details, but so be it. He would know why soon enough.

"STK. So good – one of my faves. Wish you were here."

"That would be nice, wouldn't it?" she replied. Tessa let out a sigh of relief that it had been so easy to figure out where he was, and that he wished she was there.

She immediately jumped into action and called for a cab. Flying down the elevator, she was pacing the lobby impatiently when the cab showed up five minutes later. The short ride to STK seemed too long to someone about to surprise her love after months had passed.

When the car pulled up to the entrance, Tessa paid the driver and dashed out of the car. She fidgeted with her dress and smoothed her hair, making sure everything and every hair was in place. With shoulders squared in determination, she strode purposefully through the arched trellises, taking note of the numerous paparazzi hanging around the entrance. This must be a hot spot for celebrity sightings. Tessa kept forgetting that Nate was a celebrity. She hardly ever thought of him that way.

Once inside the restaurant, she wasn't quite sure what to do next. She clearly couldn't walk up to the hostess station and ask where Nate was seated. They would never tell her, and it would look like something a crazy fan would do. She peered around, trying to be nonchalant as she figured out her next step.

STK was dimly lit and cozy, exuding chic finesse and a seductive atmosphere. Tessa wasn't surprised that a place like this was a celebrity favorite. Everything in the space screamed luxury.

After a moment of pondering, Tessa decided to go to the bar, have a drink and hope that she would be able to spot Nate from there. Fate was on her side, though. On her way to the bar situated across the large room, she spotted him.

Her heart leapt inside her chest before it took a quick spiral down into the pit of her stomach. Nate wasn't alone. From her position, he was facing her, talking to a blonde seated across from him. He didn't see Tessa, but Tessa had a front-row view as the blonde reached across the table to hold Nate's hand as Nate smiled and nodded.

Frozen where she stood, Tessa willed herself to spin around and hurry out of the restaurant before Nate could see her. But, it was too late. Just as she was turning to leave, Nate caught sight of her. Surprise registered on his face.

"Tessa!" he called out and jumped up from his seat. Tessa shook her head at him and hurried outside. She didn't want to hear whatever he had to say. Clearly, Nate had moved on. She'd seen it with her own eyes.

What made it worse, Nate had just said that he'd wished she was there. Tessa wasn't about to rekindle anything with someone else's man. On top of that, Nate wasn't being true to this blonde girlfriend of his. Tessa would have been livid if she found out her boyfriend was texting another girl while on a date with her.

Poor girl. Her problem though, not mine, she thought sadly. With heavy steps, Tessa walked back through the lovely arches. Midway down the walk, the paparazzi jumped into action – snapping pictures and calling out, "Nate! Nate! Hey, man! Picture please! Look this way? How are things with Ansley?"

All of the commotion stunned Tessa. The atmosphere had gone from peaceful stillness to flashing frenzy in two seconds flat. She felt someone pull her arm, and turned around to see who had touched her.

"What do you want?" she snapped when she saw that it was Nate.

"Tessa, what are you doing here?" he asked, not caring that they were being crowded in by paparazzi.

"I came to surprise you, but *obviously* you are tied up at the moment, so I'll just go away," Tessa said, her voice cracking.

"Can we go somewhere," Nate glanced around as cameras whirred, "a little more private to talk?"

"What is there to say?" she asked, hurt dripping in her voice. Tessa hated that she'd been so wrong in coming here.

"*Obviously,* a lot. And I'm not letting you leave this time," he said. "Come with me, I have a private car waiting around back." Nate put his arm around Tessa and shielded her from the crazed cameramen. Tessa was sure they were getting their fill of pricey images with the show she and Nate had just inadvertently provided.

She wasn't sure if she wanted to go with Nate, but it was a better alternative compared to the prospect of being followed by paparazzi as she called and waited for another cab. Plus, he wasn't giving her an option. He led her back through the restaurant as dozens of eyes bore holes into them. Tessa had a feeling she and Nate were going to be plastered on tabloids, newspapers and online gossip columns the next day.

Nate opened a side door that went down a flight of steps and into a private parking deck. Thankfully, no paparazzi were lurking. He motioned for the attendant to pull his car around, and the sharply dressed guy gave a nod and took off running. These people took their valet services seriously, she supposed.

As they waited for the car, Tessa and Nate stood there in awkward silence. Tessa wasn't sure how to proceed. The evening had taken a turn that she never would've expected – even in her most outlandish dreams.

The black sports car was pulled around promptly, and Nate held the door open for Tessa to slide onto the seat. He tipped the attendant, got in and took off quickly. Barely a moment passed before he spoke.

"Tessa, while I'm beyond happy to see you, I don't think you have any idea what you've just done," Nate said, staring straight ahead.

"Oh, so sorry. That blonde will be pretty pissed that I ruined y'all's date," Tessa replied, her words drenched in sarcasm. Nate turned to look at her, his eyes wide.

"Do you think that I was on a date?" he asked incredulously.

"Who wouldn't think you were on a date?" she shot back.

"I know there are rumors about Ansley and me, but that's all they are – rumors. We were having dinner together because we're friends and we have scenes to reshoot later this evening."

"Nate, I'm sure everyone in that restaurant thought the same thing that I did – that you were on a date with her."

"Tessa, you have to understand. If people see us together and come to their own conclusions – it helps sell movies. The producers ask us to hang out from time to time to keep the public intrigued. Never at any point have Ansley and I ever been anything more than friends. I promise."

Tessa shook her head, annoyed with herself. "Nate, I'm so sorry for jumping to conclusions and acting like a crazed, jealous girlfriend. If you were on a date, you would have every right to be. I was the one that ended things the way I did, and I owe you an apology for that, too."

They pulled into a private drive and Nate punched in a gate code.

"Where are we?" Tessa asked.

"My house. I can take you back to wherever you are staying, but it's safer and more private here for the moment. Is this okay?"

Tessa nodded her head. She was still pretty shaken up by the whole experience. A private, gated home seemed like a good idea.

"Plus, I think we have a lot that still needs to be talked about, and unlike the last time, I'm not going to let you storm out of my life without me even realizing what happened," he added.

"I definitely need to explain all of that," Tessa said sheepishly.

Nate gave her hand a squeeze after he had parked in the garage. It was getting dark, and Tessa couldn't really make out what Nate's house looked like – just that it was big and angular with a white stucco finish. Definitely a house you would never see in Clearhill.

"Don't you have to work tonight?" she asked.

Nate looked at the time. "I need to leave in a few minutes, but I shouldn't be all night. Will you wait for me here until I get back? It's more comfortable than a hotel room, and it will give us a chance to sort everything out. Please stay," he said and touched her hand. How could she not? Wasn't this why she was here?

"Okay. I won't make the same mistake. I'll stay," she promised.

Nate got out of the car and walked around and opened Tessa's door. He took her hand in his as they walked together to the door.

"Welcome to my home, Tessa," he said as he opened the door and allowed her to step inside first. The lights automatically came on, soft and soothing, in the kitchen where they'd entered. Everything was sleek and modern, but relaxing. Glossy granite countertops, slick white cabinets and ultra-technical appliances surrounded by lots of large glass windows made up the kitchen.

"Do you cook a lot in here?" she asked as she looked around.

"Some. Not much – it's just me here," he admitted as he tossed his keys and jacket on the table.

"Everything is so...pristine," Tessa said when the word finally came to her. The house was huge and the complete opposite of her cramped, cozy apartment.

"I can't really take the credit for that – I have a cleaning service. Do you want something to drink?" he asked.

"Water would be nice."

Nate took two bottles of water from the fridge, handed one to Tessa and motioned for her to follow him. "Let me show you around before I have to leave," he said as he stepped into the living room.

A marble fireplace and built-ins flanked one wall of the spacious room that housed two large leather sofas and a sheepskin rug that looked so soft Tessa thought she could curl up and take a nap on it.

Nate took her around the house before finishing up the tour back in the living room.

"You have a nice home, Nate. Thanks for inviting me here," Tessa said with her hands clasped in front of her.

"Well, I sort of just brought you here without even telling you this was where we were going, so thank you for trusting me. I'm glad you're here in my home, and that you're staying."

Tessa smiled. There was so much to say, but it would have to wait until he returned. She took the two steps to cover the space between them, and put her arms around his neck, hugging him tightly. "Me, too. I know you have to go, but I'm already counting the minutes until you get back."

Nate wrapped her in his arms and kissed her forehead. "I am, too."

She looked up and he softly kissed her lips. The kiss was short and sweet, but it awakened a fire that had been simmering within her for months. She'd forgotten how intense their physical connection was.

"Hurry back," she whispered, moving from his embrace.

Nate looked at her longingly, but knowing that she was right, he did need to go, said goodbye and hurried to leave before he changed his mind.

***

Tessa's eyes looked over the top of the book she was reading when she heard Nate unlocking the door. Curled up in a chair wearing Nate's sweatshirt and a pair of his boxers that she'd found, she'd been trying to stay awake after he'd left for the studio to shoot scenes.

Nate told her that she had free rein of his home, but her heart was still soaring from the too short, but blissful, moments they'd spent together, and she had far too much on her mind to sleep. So, she'd found an interesting book and settled into a big, cozy chair to wait for Nate's return.

When he rounded the corner and she caught her first glimpse of him in the darkened doorway, the huge smile on her face vanished.

"What's wrong?" she asked, alarmed.

Nate shook his head and ran his hands through his hair as he entered the room. "We have a problem. I'm so sorry, Tessa."

Tessa's mind immediately jumped to the worst conclusion, as it had a tendency to do in most matters as of late, but she took a deep breath to steady herself before her emotions went into overdrive without knowing the reason. "What's going on?"

Nate flopped onto the sofa. "The press situation is about a thousand times worse than I'd anticipated. Instead of the story spinning that I might be seeing someone unknown, which would have put us in the spotlight for a bit, but it would've been manageable, the press has rumors swirling that I've cheated on Ansley, left her brokenhearted and taken up with a mystery girl."

Tessa sat in stunned silence as Nate put his head in his hands.

"So the whole world will see me as a mistress and you as a cheater?"

"It's so frustrating, Tessa! Ansley and I are good friends – we always have been. But, to sell movies and make our publicists happy, we've let the press make their own assumptions about us and never disputed anything, and now it has come back to bite me. Hard."

"Do you think it will affect your career?" Tessa asked. This whole thing was surreal, and she couldn't yet grasp that her face would be plastered on tabloids and magazines, painted in a negative light, for weeks to come. Right now, she just felt the need to calm Nate down.

"I don't know. My agent says not to worry, that bad publicity is still publicity, and since I'm so quiet about my private life, this may end up being a good thing. I don't so much care about all of that as much as I care about how this will affect you. You're going to be hounded. When you get back home, the paparazzi will be waiting and watching your every move."

"There isn't all that much to see. I'm sure they will get bored pretty fast."

"I wish that were true. You have no idea what these people are capable of. I'm going to worry nonstop about you. I know we haven't had a chance to have a conversation about this, but if we're going to pursue a relationship, would you ever consider moving here to LA?"

Tessa's jaw dropped. What was it with men asking her to pick up and move lately? "Nate, it's not that I wouldn't consider moving here, I'm willing to do whatever it takes to make this work, but I don't have a job or a place to live and I don't know anyone other than you. Would you ever consider moving to Clearhill?"

She had turned the tables and put the pressure back on Nate. They hadn't even had a chance to discuss their relationship yet, and he was already asking her to move. Not that she would totally be opposed, but she needed to know where things stood first.

"I would absolutely consider moving there – just like you, I'm willing to do whatever it takes. As far as a job goes, you are a fantastic writer, and I have plenty of contacts – publishing companies, screenwriters, magazine editors, so if that's your hang-up, it could easily be solved."

Tessa hadn't heard much after Nate had said he was willing to move to Clearhill for her without batting an eye. If she had had any doubts about Nate's feelings, they were now obliterated.

"I think we have some things that need discussing before we jump into either of us moving across the country," Tessa said.

"I agree. We need to talk."

Now that the moment of truth was here, Tessa felt at a loss for words. Where should she start? There was so much to say. They both sat in silence for a moment, neither exactly sure where to start.

"I want to tell you again how happy I am that you came here, Tessa," Nate said, breaking the silence.

"I'm glad I did, too. I know I've apologized for jumping to conclusions back when everything happened, but there is so much more for me to explain."

"You can tell me anything."

"When we first started seeing each other, I fell for you – there is no doubt about it. And to be honest, I haven't stopped thinking about you since we first met. But, I'd just come out of a relationship that had ended with me getting my heart broken. When what was happening between us escalated so quickly, it scared me, and I took the first opportunity I had to stupidly end it. I didn't want to get hurt again, and I just assumed that was what would happen when you left after your movie was finished shooting.

"Plus, I was afraid that since one man had already told me that long-distance relationships never worked, I figured there was no point in dragging out what would eventually end. I was falling so hard for you..."

"Tessa, I fell in love with you. I said it months ago, and my feelings haven't changed. I haven't stopped thinking about you, trying to figure out how much space I needed to give you – when it would be best to contact you. Did you get the flowers I sent you?"

Tessa smiled. "Yes, I did, and they were beautiful. To be honest, at first I thought that they were from Davis, since he had come back into town and had asked me to move to Nashville with him, but, don't worry, that wasn't going to happen. I figured out pretty quick that my heart belonged to someone other than him. That's why I'm here."

Nate stood up and took Tessa's hands in his, pulling her up into his arms. "You are it for me, girl. There is no doubt about it," he whispered with his forehead against hers. His words were straightforward. He wasn't messing around.

She gazed up into Nate's eyes, looking into love and adoration that made her feel warm and content. She returned his gaze, hoping he felt the intensity of her love for him, as well. After locking eyes, sharing intimate feelings that couldn't be conveyed with words, he kissed her. This second kiss was full of hope and promises.

Big Love in a Small Town

This was it. She'd never felt this way before, and Tessa knew she would never feel this way about anyone else. It didn't matter where they lived, what they did, who they were – as long as she was with Nate, everything would be alright. She rested her head against his shoulder as they held each other, swaying back and forth to the symphony of love that permeated the air. It was impossible to keep still when their hearts were singing with the joy of reuniting and discovering that they both knew they were meant for each other.

Chapter 7

Still locked in the embrace of reunited love, Tessa wanted the moment to never end. She was in Nate's arms where she belonged, and she didn't plan on ever leaving. Nate leaned down and rested his cheek against hers. Even in this joyous moment, she could tell something was still bothering him.

"Is the rumor thing still on your mind?" she asked.

He sighed. "Yes, I'm sorry, but it is. I don't want it to ruin this moment with you – I'm just worried. Not about me, but about you. I wanted to protect you from all of that, and it ended up being a problem right off of the bat."

"I'm not going to sweat it, Nate. Who cares what people that we don't even know think about us? We know the truth, and I'm sure Ansley will back your story up. There isn't a need to hide away. I'm not ashamed of loving you, and this mess won't make me stop. Nothing will ever make me stop loving you," she said with intensity.

Nate brushed his fingertips against her cheek, admiring her courage and fierce devotion. "I'm glad to hear that's how you feel, but some of these people are relentless. A good portion of the press are kind and respectful, but there are quite a few bad apples that spoil the bunch. They will follow you everywhere, asking questions, getting in your business and driving you crazy."

"Whatever comes, I think I can handle it. Don't worry so much, Nate. I know you're famous – I've always known that. The gossip and tabloids are just part of the package, and I'm willing to deal with it." She winked at him. "I guess you're worth it."

Nate laughed, and the hearty sound was music to Tessa's ears. She didn't want him stressing out any more than necessary about the press. It wasn't worth wasting extra energy worrying about something neither of them could change.

Smiling up at his much happier face, Tessa said, "I love you, Nate, and everything will be fine."

He pulled her close. "I love you, too, and the way that you're taking this all in stride makes me feel much better."

"Good. I'm glad. So why don't we go to bed and take some time to just...not think anymore?" Tessa asked.

"I'd love to...not think anymore. I've wanted to not think anymore with you all night," Nate said in jest, but his eyes smoldered with serious want.

When their lips met in a searing kiss, all thoughts and worries vanished. Nothing but the taste of Nate's lips on hers and his fingertips tracing lightly down her back mattered. Nate and Tessa managed to make it to his bedroom, shedding clothes and bumping into walls in the frenzy that had overtaken them.

Slipping into the sheets, Tessa broke away from Nate's kiss to study him. She took her time appraising his piercing blue eyes, his dark brows, and the five o'clock shadow that covered his strong jawline. She caressed his face in her hands. "Let's savor each second – every kiss, every touch. I don't ever want to forget this night," she whispered.

Nate seemed to study her, as well, nodding his agreement before he leaned down to claim her lips once more. He spent the rest of the dark morning hours making love to Tessa in his bed, adoring every inch of her to the point that he even planted kisses behind her knees and in the crooks of her elbows.

They couldn't get enough of one another, and made sure to draw out every moment, lingering as long as possible with every single touch and caress.

Love drunk and finally sated, with the sound of Nate's heart pounding beneath her ear, Tessa glimpsed out the large windows. The view from Nate's bedroom showed the sky turning from a soft, faded pink to a fiery, golden orange as the sun rose. As she watched the glorious sunrise, the only sounds she could hear were the two of them still trying to catch their breath. Still lying on top of Nate's chest, her body was languid and her limbs felt like jelly. When she finally mustered enough energy to move, she repositioned herself, curling up against Nate as he pulled the bedcovers over them.

The last thing she remembered before her eyes could no longer stay open and she drifted off into a dreamless sleep was Nate whispering, "I love you, Tessa. I knew even from the moment we met that I would love you."

***

Despite being exhausted from his busy day and his time with Tessa, Nate stayed awake long after she'd fallen asleep. He was worried. He'd put the feelings aside to focus on Tessa, and to keep her from catching on to just how much of a concern he felt this warranted. Those things could wait until she had slept, but the conversation he'd had with his agent earlier about the current press problem wasn't something that he could easily cast aside.

Tessa had acted so nonchalant about the rumors, but Nate knew that it was going to be a lot worse than she was expecting. He wanted to be prepared to be whatever support she might need. He would be there for her, and he wasn't going anywhere. They would make it through this. Nate was determined to see their fledgling relationship through the worst of the media storm that was about to batter them.

Nate hadn't spent the last couple of months with Tessa occupying his every waking thought and haunting his dreams to let her slip through his hands because of this. What he and Tessa had shared when he had been filming in Georgia had changed everything for him. He'd heard it before, and now knew it was true – love wasn't so much about time. Sometimes, you just knew when it was right, and Nate knew that he and Tessa belonged together. He just knew.

When she had shown up at STK last night, Nate's heart had soared. He hadn't thought twice about the press surrounding them – all he could focus on was keeping Tessa from leaving him again. That was his sole priority, getting her to stay. If he'd been thinking, he would have tried to keep their interactions even more private than he had.

Thankfully, Tessa was a part of his life again, and as she sighed and snuggled up against him, Nate silently vowed to protect her from the slew of press that he knew she wouldn't be ready to face. The press could be ruthless, and they could push and ask questions that were downright heartless.

Nate didn't feel comfortable with Tessa leaving for Georgia in a couple of days without him. After pondering his options as the morning light filtered into his bedroom, he knew what he had to do. He was going to clear his schedule and go back home with her. That was all there was to it.

They would have to work out details, but if it ended up that he had to move to Georgia, then he would just move to Georgia. Whatever he needed to do, he was going to do it to make their relationship work. Bottom line.

***

"Well, are you all packed?" Tessa asked Nate three days later. She still couldn't believe he was flying back to Georgia with her. Even though she'd tried her best to insist that he didn't have to go with her, Nate wasn't taking no for an answer and Tessa, while not making a big deal about the press, was secretly glad that she wasn't having to tell him goodbye.

"Packed and ready. Are you?"

Tessa surveyed her luggage, mentally checking everything off of her list. Nate had his assistant go over to Tessa's hotel to collect her things and bring them back to his house.

"Yep, all set."

"The driver's ready."

When the private car was loaded and they were seated, holding hands, as they headed down the short, but private, drive, Tessa leaned her head against the black leather seat and reflected over the past couple of days.

They hadn't left Nate's house – they'd simply spent the past few days in their own private bubble with no outside worries or concerns. They'd enjoyed spending every second with each other, whether it was listening to music and sipping wine, making love in the heated pool, or just watching a movie cuddled on the sofa. It had been the perfect respite from the rest of the world.

But, as the gate to Nate's drive opened, Tessa realized that the rest of the world was waiting impatiently for them to reenter it. Dozens of paparazzi flanked either side of the curb as the skilled driver managed to maneuver his way out. Tessa swallowed. Nate hadn't been kidding – this was a little much.

"This is nothing," Nate murmured, leaning in close to her, subconsciously trying to shield her.

"Nothing?" Tessa queried, her voice quivering with nerves.

"Yeah, sometimes it can get really out of hand, but everyone seems to be mindful today, and they stayed out of the driver's way."

Tessa observed the crowd of cameramen, furiously snapping pictures and waving. They must have been camped out by the gate – waiting, knowing that at some point, Nate would have to leave with his "mystery woman" in tow.

"Why isn't there a law against that kind of stuff, like a privacy law or something?"

"Even though it can be frustrating, the entertainment industry needs them snapping pictures and inadvertently promoting celebrities. Fans want to see pictures and read stories about their favorites. They wouldn't be camped out by my gate if the story and the pictures wouldn't sell."

Tessa contemplated what Nate was saying. It made sense, but it still didn't make it any easier to get used to the idea of so many people being interested in her. Her musings were interrupted when she heard Nate's phone vibrate.

"Thank God," he said as he read the text message he'd just received. Relief flooded his face.

"Good news?" she ventured.

"The best. Ansley just told me that she released a statement through her publicist that said we are only close friends, and that she wished me every happiness. She even closed it with saying that she couldn't wait to meet my new girlfriend."

"Oh, that is good news."

"Yep. A lot of fans that hoped we were seeing each other in real life will be disappointed, but it's better than everyone thinking that I cheated on her. Both of our agents and publicists agreed. We have a movie coming out in a few months, so hopefully the ripple will have smoothed over by then."

Tessa squeezed his hand. "I'm sure it will, everything will be fine. We've got each other, and all the details will keep falling into place, sweetheart."

Nate kissed her temple. "I love you, you know that?"

"I had a feeling you did."

"Okay. Good."

***

"What in the world is going on, Tessa?" Mr. Hart asked, hurrying to her when she managed to break through the crowd and get into the newspaper office, locking the door behind her. She hadn't expected her first day back at work to be like this. Thinking maybe a few paparazzi might show up, she'd driven to work instead of walking, but the crowd of twenty or so cameramen that swarmed her car and surrounded her for the short walk to the front door had caught her off guard.

"I'm sorry, Mr. Hart. I had no idea it would be this bad," she said as she set her bag and keys down on her desk. The phone was ringing furiously.

"That thing has been ringing off of the hook for days. People wanting to know if you work here, where you live, who your parents are, if you are seeing some guy."

"All of this is because I am seeing a guy. But he isn't just any guy, as I'm sure you've figured out. It's Nate Wilder, and we are more than just seeing each other – this is the real thing."

"While I'm glad to hear that you're happy, this concerns me, Tessa. We are just a small-town newspaper – I'm not sure if we can handle the flood of inquiries coming in. Have they bothered you at home?"

"Not really. They can't trespass on private property. I've had a few stragglers hang out near the street, but since the drive is long, and there isn't much to see, I think they all figured that it would be more productive to wait for me here. This will die down in a few days – the story is just breaking, so everyone wants to know about me right now, but once the novelty has worn off, I think things will go back to normal."

Mr. Hart eyed her skeptically. "I may be an old man, but if you are going to share your life with a celebrity, I don't think you can ever expect things to go back to your version of normal."

Tessa glanced through the glass door at the crowd still hovering outside. Mr. Hart was right. The press would lose a good bit of interest in her once the newness of her and Nate together wore off, but as long as she was with him, she would stay on their radar.

"I'm sorry if this causes issues for the newspaper. I didn't expect this many people to be here."

"Tessa, we're a newspaper – we are the press. I'm not worried about the interest – I just want you to be okay. I may be your boss, but I've known you since you were a little girl, and your well-being is what's most important to me. If you need to take a leave of absence, you can do that."

"I don't know what will happen, but that means a lot, Mr. Hart."

"I think it's best if you take today off. I don't think you would be able to get much work done with all those folks trying to stare at you through the door," Mr. Hart said while gesturing to the onlookers peering in through the glass door.

"You'd think people would have better things to do..." Tessa mumbled, but she knew he was right.

"Do you have someone that could pick you up? Should we call Chief Allen and get a police escort over here?"

"No, that's not needed. I haven't had anyone threaten my safety. I'll call someone to come pick me up, though. It might be overwhelming trying to get back home by myself."

"Good idea, Tessa. That makes me feel much better."

Tessa grabbed her phone out of her purse and dialed Nate's number.

"Hey, Tessa, what's up?" he answered.

"I've got a situation. The press are here swarming, and Mr. Hart thinks it's best that I take the day off. Do you mind coming to get me? I don't feel comfortable leaving alone."

"I'll be there in five minutes. Is there another entrance? It would be best if your boss can escort you out when I pull up. If I'm seen, the situation will just get worse."

"There's a back door facing the alley – don't pull your car in there or you'll get stuck. I'll meet you. Just text me."

She hung up with Nate, and explained to Mr. Hart what they needed to do.

A few minutes later when Tessa got the text from Nate, she and Mr. Hart sprang into action, hurrying through the back door and down the three hundred or so feet of alleyway to the street where Nate's car sat waiting.

Tessa jumped into the passenger seat after giving her boss a quick hug. As soon as she shut her door, Nate started moving, and Tessa breathed a sigh of relief that her exit had gone off without a hitch.

"Tessa, I hate to say it, but I think you may have to consider working from home for a while," Nate said as he drove back towards Tessa's apartment. He was wearing a ball cap and dark shades.

"Nate, I don't like skulking around. This really sucks," Tessa said with conviction.

"Trust me, I know it does. But, this won't last forever. As soon as a more interesting story hits, the swarm of media will be over."

"I've read magazines, watched E! News and clicked on the online stories. People want to know everything about you. They can't get enough. Clearhill is pretty used to celebrities because of all the movies filmed here, and the citizens usually don't bother the sets and stuff, but if you are just going to be out and about with me on a regular basis, even they are going to notice," Tessa told him.

They pulled into her drive and got out, the conversation on hold for a moment. She scurried up the steps, knowing somewhere near the street, a lens was surely zooming in, hoping to snap a newsworthy shot of either her or Nate.

Once inside, she sat at the kitchen table and motioned for Nate to join her. He took a seat, removed his glasses and hat, and took her hand that was resting on the table.

Big Love in a Small Town

"What are we going to do?" she asked, her eyes searching Nate's face.

"Whatever it takes," he replied.

"I know that – we've figured that part out, but I mean literally. What are we going to do? What's our next step?"

"To be honest, Tessa, I don't think me in LA and you being here is going to work. It just isn't."

Tessa felt like the wind was knocked out of her. Was he already calling it quits? How could she have been so wrong about what was happening between them? She thought they were both in it forever.

"What are you saying?" she managed to squeak out. Nate's eyes grew wide and he shook his head furiously.

"Oh no. No – not what you are thinking. I'm not saying we shouldn't be together. I'm saying we should be together. We need to live in the same place. I know it seems crazy and so soon, but that isn't how it feels to me. It feels right. I'll move here if you want me to, or you are welcome to move to LA and live with me. Wherever you choose. It's your choice."

"So you're saying that you want us to move in together?" Tessa had to make sure that she was getting this right.

"Yes, but if you aren't comfortable with that, I can get a place nearby, or we could find somewhere in LA for you."

Tessa mulled over her options. Never in her wildest dreams had she ever considered moving to Los Angeles – and moving in with someone was such a big step. Plus, what would her parents and Natalie say?

She'd just told her parents about Nate, and it had freaked them out. They were worried. Tessa knew they would flip if she told them that she was moving, but Natalie would probably wish her the best and tell her to go for it.

There were more opportunities for her career, also, if she moved to Los Angeles. But on the other hand, Clearhill was home with its oak-lined streets, antebellum homes and historic square. She loved Clearhill and its residents.

"I'm going to have to take some time to make this decision, Nate."

"I know – it's a big step. Take as much time as you need. It's easier for me to do whatever you decide – whether we live here or in LA. A lot of movies are shot on location now and I can keep my home in LA for when I do need to spend extended time there. Plus, my mom lives in New York and Dad lives in Denver, so I don't have any family there."

"But I know it's good for you to be in LA. I'm going to take this all into consideration. You need to fly back Wednesday, right?"

"Yes, I can't put off shooting the rest of my scenes any longer or the director is going to explode," he said sheepishly.

"I'm going to stay here for a couple of extra days to gather my thoughts, and I'll fly out over the weekend. I need to really think."

"I understand. Will you at least let me hire security? They won't bother you – they'll just follow you at a safe distance. It'll make me feel so much better about leaving you."

"If that will make you feel better, you can hire security."

Chapter 8

When her plane touched down in Los Angeles Friday evening, Tessa was beyond ready to see Nate. She had missed him so much over the past two days. So many couples, when she interviewed them for their engagement announcements, had told her, "You just know, when you've met the one, you just know," and she now, finally, knew what they meant.

A driver was waiting for her just outside of baggage claim, holding up a sign with her name on it. Tessa frowned. She thought Nate was coming to pick her up.

Slightly disappointed, Tessa let the chauffeur take her bags and she followed him to the waiting vehicle. He opened the trunk of a black limousine and placed her bags inside before opening the door for her.

The limo took Tessa by surprise. It was a luxurious gesture on Nate's part. He usually drove himself or hired a simple town car. Tessa wasn't going to complain, though. She sank back against the leather seats and took in her surroundings. That's when she saw the lovely bouquet of ivory roses and lilies sitting on the side seat with a card tucked among the blooms.

She picked up the flowers as the limo pulled away from the curb. Inhaling the sweet fragrance, Tessa pulled out the note and read it.

Big Love in a Small Town

Sweet Tessa,

I've missed you. Crazy that it's been only two days. It feels like it's been much longer. I know you were expecting me at the airport, but I promise, I'll see you soon. I have a special evening planned for us, so just sit back, have a glass of wine and enjoy the ride.

I love you.

Nate

Tessa pressed the note against her chest. How was it possible that she was living out her own personal fairy tale? How did she get so lucky? This wonderful man was treating her like a princess, and she couldn't wait to wrap her arms around him and tell him what she'd decided.

After pouring herself a glass of wine, just as Nate had instructed, she leaned back and savored the first sip of her favorite brand of pinot noir. Tessa smiled – he'd stocked the limo with her favorite flowers and her favorite wine.

As they continued to drive, Tessa wondered where she was going. The road wasn't familiar and they'd been on it a while. It didn't seem to be in the direction of Nate's house – the route was coastal, and she was pretty sure it was Pacific Coast Highway.

Twenty minutes later, they pulled into a short, gated drive. The gate opened, and the driver pulled up next to a glass, wood and concrete contemporary beach house. A good glance around told Tessa that they were in Malibu.

With her bags in tow, the driver showed Tessa to the gorgeous home's front door and opened it for her. Inside, the lights were dim, candles were flickering and cream rose petals were scattered in a trail down the wide hall.

"I was told to tell you to follow the rose petals," the driver said with a smile before letting himself out.

Tessa eagerly followed the trail as it wound around the corner, through the kitchen, and to the back door. When she opened the door and stepped onto the large deck, she paused her quest momentarily to take in the breathtaking view. The sun was setting, and as it sank slowly towards the ocean, the sky was set ablaze with shades of pink, orange and smoky gray.

"Wow," she said under her breath. A warm breeze caused her skirt to flow and a couple of petals blew against her sandaled feet. Getting back on task, Tessa continued following the petals down the plank steps that led to the wide expanse of beach.

That's when she saw him. Standing with his back to the ocean, dressed in linen pants and a white shirt, Nate was waiting for her. The trail of rose petals led to an elegant, white table set for two not far from where Nate stood, but Tessa only had eyes for him. She broke into a run and leapt into his arms.

"I'm so happy to see you!" she said as she hugged him tightly.

"I've missed you," he whispered against her hair as he swirled her around before kissing her deeply.

"You are really spoiling me, you know that, right?" she teased after he'd put her down.

"You deserve it. I want to do these things for you," he told her as he led her to a seat at the table.

After she sat down, he took his seat and poured them each a glass of champagne.

"Where are we exactly?" Tessa asked as she picked up her glass.

"Funny you should ask…" Nate trailed off as he lifted his own champagne. "To wonderful beginnings," he toasted and they each took a sip of the sparkling wine.

"So, I'm terrible at suspense. What have you decided?" Nate asked after he'd lifted the silver lids, revealing elegantly plated grilled shrimp and angel hair pasta.

"No subtlety, huh?" Tessa said, smiling at him as she took another sip.

"Nope. I'm interested to find out where I'll be living."

Tessa sat the champagne flute on the white linen tablecloth. She took Nate's hand in hers. "I'm ready to take this jump, Nate. I'm going to move to LA. I don't have details worked out, and as much as I love you, I think it may be a bit too early for us to move in together."

Nate nodded, a smile spreading across his face. "I hoped you would choose LA. There are so many opportunities here. Plus, we will buy a house in Clearhill, and you can visit as often and as long as you like."

He leaned over and kissed her on the cheek. "While I would be perfectly happy if you moved in with me, I had a feeling you might not be ready for that. If it's alright with you, I have a house where you can live until we decide to take the next step."

"And where is this other house of yours?" Tessa laughed. "Connected to your pool?"

"Why? Do you prefer waterfront?" he asked.

"I'm just kidding, Nate. I don't expect you to provide me with a house."

"But, I already have a house, so it's not a big deal. Will you at least think about it?"

"I'll think about it. Where is it? I'm not very familiar with the area, so I'd hoped to find something close to you or downtown."

Nate looked toward the house that she'd come through to get to the beach. "Right there."

Tessa's jaw dropped. "You can't be serious, Nate."

"I'm very serious. It's my beach house. Well, it's your beach house for as long as you want to call it that. I figured it would be nice to write on the deck with the waves in the background."

Tears pooled in Tessa's eyes. "How am I so lucky?"

Nate brushed away the tear that had fallen onto her cheek. Before she knew what was happening, he had gotten on his knee by her chair, her hand clasped in his.

"Tessa, when I'm in, I'm all in. For the long haul. Forever. Some may think I'm crazy – hell, you may think I'm crazy – but when you know, you know. And I know you are meant for me. I'm in love with you – committed, never leaving your side, you are my world.

"I know what it is to have had you in my life, and then not had you. I don't ever want to feel that way again, and I will spend every day for the rest of forever making sure you know how much I love you. What I'm about to ask you is for the future, for a time when we both feel it's right, but I want to ask you now as a pledge, a vow to you that I cherish you and what we have together, and I always will.

"Will you please do me the honor of becoming my wife?" Nate pulled a brilliant, sparkling diamond ring from his pocket and held it out to her. Was this really happening? Was she dreaming?

"Nate, I love you. I made some mistakes, I pushed you away, and you welcomed me back with open arms, completely embracing me. You're right, some may think it's crazy. If you would have told me this a month ago, I would have believed it was crazy. But, I know you're it for me, too. This is love, babe, and I can't wait to one day be your wife. I want to be with you forever. So, the answer is yes, a thousand times, yes!"

Nate slipped the ring on her finger and she wrapped her arms around him, kissing him soundly. He scooped her up, twirling her around in the twilight as the waves broke against the shore. Perfection, Tessa thought. This moment was perfection. A perfect fairy tale with a whirlwind ending, that wasn't really the end, but the beginning.

The day she met Nate months ago was a day that had started with a heart still broken and tears still falling. But, it had led to this night – a night of joy and love and beaches with stars twinkling happily over the horizon. She couldn't have imagined in her wildest dreams that this would have happened, and surely Nate hadn't expected to meet his future wife in a little Southern town. Neither of them had expected to fall in love so completely with one another to the point that any other option than together forever, well, simply wasn't an option.

One Last Thing…

If you believe that *Big Love in a Small Town* is worth sharing, would you spend a minute to let your friends know about it?

If this book lets them have a great time, they will be enormously grateful to you – as will I.

Kate

www.KateGoldmanBooks.com

About Kate Goldman

In childhood I observed a huge love between my mother and father and promised myself that one day I would meet a man whom I would fall in love with head over heels. At the age of 16, I wrote my first romance story that was published in a student magazine and was read by my entire neighborhood. I enjoy writing romance stories that readers can turn into captivating imaginary movies where characters fall in love, overcome difficult obstacles, and participate in best adventures of their lives. Most of the time you can find me reading a great fiction book in a cozy armchair, writing a romance story in a hammock near the ocean, or traveling around the world with my beloved husband.

In Love With a Haunted House

The last thing Mallory Clark wants to do is move back home. She has no choice, though, since the company she worked for in Chicago has just downsized her, and everybody else. To make matters worse her fiancé has broken their engagement, and her heart, leaving her hurting and scarred. When her mother tells her that the house she always coveted as a child, the once-famed Gray Oaks Manor, is not only on the market but selling for a song, it seems to Mallory that the best thing she could possibly do would be to put Chicago, and everything and everyone in it, behind her. Arriving back home she runs into gorgeous and mysterious Blake Hunter. Blake is new to town and like her he is interested in buying the crumbling old Victorian on the edge of the historic downtown center, although his reasons are his own. Blake is instantly intrigued by the flame-haired beauty with the fiery temper and the vulnerable expression in her eyes. He can feel the attraction between them and knows it is mutual, but he also knows that the last thing on earth he needs is to get involved with a woman determined to take away a house he has to have.

The Sheikh's Girlfriend

Tara coughs from sand in her mouth and realizes that the plane in which she was traveling to Omani just crash-landed in the middle of the desert. A group of nomads get into the plane, however instead of helping passengers, they steal jewelry and kidnap young women, including Tara's sister. Just after the nomads leave, another group of men led by a handsome sheikh, Sofian, arrives to rescue the passengers. Tara is grateful for Sofian's help but they quickly get off on the wrong foot as their personalities clash. Sofian is used to doing things his way and to speaking only to his family members or people who he gives orders to. He gets irritated by Tara as she is always speaking to him about her sister and asking too many questions. Tara notices that Sofian is closed off and cold but tries to find out why he is the way he is and likes the person she discovers underneath that tough exterior. Even though their characters clash and she annoys him, Sofian falls in love with Tara. She is different from everybody he knows. Sofian has been chasing nomads that have been kidnapping tourists for a while, but now it is time to put a stop to all of it once and for all. He makes an even bigger effort to rescue Tara's sister but after he finds her, how will he let Tara go back to the U.S.? He can't imagine life without her.

.

Love for Dessert

When Anastasia Emmott learns of her best friend's engagement, she hopes that her own boyfriend of three years will propose. But instead of giving her a ring, he breaks her heart by leaving her for another woman two weeks before their anniversary. If that wasn't bad enough, Anastasia receives news that she may be demoted to a terrible position in her accounting firm. She decides that finally, she needs change in her life. She quits her job and, much to the chagrin of her mother, starts up her very own bakery. After several disastrous dates, Anastasia begins to realize that the dating game is much harder than it used to be. But when Anastasia's best friend, Ariana, pushes her to enter a baking contest, she meets Darren King, a handsome baker who has just started at the competing bakery across the street. Anastasia is swept away by his dashing good looks, charming personality and masterful baking skills. What Anastasia doesn't know is that Darren is an undercover agent, planted in the bakery to gather evidence against a drug kingpin that has been operating out of his bakery. When Anastasia becomes involved by accident and her name is put on the hit list of the city's biggest drug gang, there is no one but Darren to save her.

Printed in Great Britain
by Amazon